About the Author

Lexie Winston has been an astronaut, rock star, princess and time traveller. In her dreams. But none of the dreams have lived up to what becoming an author has been like. She gets to live in a world of pure imagination, and her heroines get to do the things she's always wished she could.

When not writing books, Lexie is a mother of two gorgeous teenagers and the wife to a patient and understanding man. They live in Western Australia and are lorded over by a black toy poodle. She loves camping, reading and if her iPad was stolen, her world would explode. (It has the kindle app on it.)

And you can find all my links at

www.lexiewinston.com

<u>Also by Lexie Winston</u>

The Collectors Division

(Paranormal Reverse Harem Series)

Guardian

Guardian's Blood

Guardian Ascending

Collector's Division Omnibus

Neighpalm Industries Collective

(Enemies to Lovers Reverse Harem)

Abandoned Girl

Broken Girl

Tormented Girl

Wanted Girl

Cherished Girl

Loved Girl

Superficial Girl - Jacinta's Story Part 1

Superficial Girl - Jacinta's Story Part 2

Neighpalm Industries Collective 1-3

Neighpalm Industries Collective 4-6

Seductive Sins Collection

(Reverse Harem Series)

Glorious Gluttony

Gangs, Guns, and Glory

Galaxy Circus

(Sci-Fi Reverse Harem Series)

Apprentice

Stagehand

Whisperer

Mama - Galaxy Circus Novella

Performer

A Night Most Wicked - Galaxy Circus Novella

Broken Promises

(Dark Poly Romance Series)

Secrets Kept

Lies Untold

Trust Broken

Love Found

M.I.T.H.O.S

(Contemporary RH)

Spies Like Me

GANGS, GUNS, AND GLORY

A Tale of a Bounty Hunting Gluttony Demon

LEXIE WINSTON

Follow your dreams, you will be amazed how truly happy you are if you do.

Chapter One

"Thank you," I whisper to the FedEx guy who just handed me my parcel. He looks at me like I'm a little strange, but he waves and disappears back to his truck, while I quietly shut the door behind me.

He'd gotten a fright when I flung the door open before he even reached the top step, but I'd been tracking that sucker for days now and there was no way I wanted anyone to get to the door before me. I've been sitting as close to the door as possible without looking suspicious to anyone else. Thankfully, I had a pile of good books to read while I waited and nobody suspected a thing—not to mention I have an amazing poker face.

Tiptoeing back to the kitchen, I quietly place the box on the countertop. "Nolan!" I call out and wait for an answer, but none comes. "Louis, Carter," I shout next, hoping they don't respond. All three of them went out for a jog earlier, and I hadn't seen nor heard them come home, but I tend to get caught up in my books, so they could have, and I wouldn't have noticed, but it looks like the coast is clear.

Giggling with glee, I grab a knife and cut through the tape holding my package together. The little golden arrow on the side screams at me to hurry up and open it. I don't have to worry about the girls because Aria is at school and Zoe is at the daycare she attends three days a week. I offered to keep her home with me, but she loves going and doing all the different activities they provide and playing with her friends.

Putting the knife to the side, I peel back the lid of the box. Nestled in amongst the packaging nuts is my brand-new toy. Carefully reaching inside, I pull it out and push the packaging away. The sleek black look and feel of the product sends tingles up and down my spine. Pulling the instruction leaflet out of the packaging, I flip through it, looking at the various settings and speeds as well as how to keep it charged. I can't wait to use this little beauty.

Putting it down, I hurry over to the back door and quickly turn the lock. I don't want the boys coming home and interrupting me. I pick it up and turn it back and forth, looking at the buttons, then I press the one I need and it starts to hum.

"Oh yeah, baby, come to momma," I purr, desperate to try it out. The sound it makes sends a thrill of excitement coursing through my body.

"Glory." A voice behind me has me screaming in surprise, and as I turn, my finger presses down on the trigger.

Prongs shoot out of the gun, soaring toward my

dripping, half naked mate who only has a towel wrapped around his waist. The prongs lodge in his chest, and fifty thousand volts go barreling down the wires and into his body. Nolan grunts, and his hands convulse around the towel he was using to dry his hair before he twitches and falls to the ground in a heap. His body spasms as his eyes roll back in his head.

Screaming in panic, I run over and drop down on the floor next to him. Shit, what do I do? My heart races with terror as I try to figure out what to do. Do I remove the prongs? Is he going to fry me when I touch him? Damn it! Why didn't I read the instructions better before I picked the damn thing up? A sob leaves my mouth at the same time I hear a noise.

"Glory?" A hand touches my shoulder, and I scream again and whirl.

In the process, I lunge out with the Taser and pull the trigger again. The two stationary prongs crackle, and electricity arcs between them as I shove it in the direction of the hand. It connects with another naked chest, and with a shout, Carter goes down like a bag of shit, twitching and groaning.

"Aggghhh!" I throw the Taser away from me, and it skids across the tiles, coming to a harmless stop.

I pull at my hair, unable to decide whether or not to call an ambulance, when I hear thundering footsteps come down the stairs.

"Glory, what's wrong? Why are you screaming, my little dumpling?" Louis skids into the room. Unlike the other two, he has pants on, but his chest is bare, and his hair is dripping. His eyes widen when he sees Carter and Nolan groaning on the ground, but I stand up, prop my hands on my hips, and narrow my eyes, the previous accident forgotten in my annoyance. Those fuckers must have been in the shower together without me. They deserve to roll around on the floor in pain.

"Did you shower without me?" I demand, but he ignores the question as he watches our lovers twitch involuntarily and moan in pain.

His gaze comes back to me. "But, my little sugar cookie, you were so involved in your book you didn't even hear us come in. We thought we'd let you keep reading." He exaggerates his French accent in an attempt to distract me because he knows it gets me all hot and bothered.

Max comes running in from wherever he was and starts to smother Carter with kisses, bathing him in slobber, which he is unable to do anything about due to his muscles still not cooperating with him. I don't intervene. I'm annoyed and disappointed. My mates are a feast for the senses, and I can't get enough of them. The gluttonous side of me is pissed off.

Turning, I flounce back, pick up my new toy, and take it to the counter before placing it next to the box.

"What… the… fuck?" Nolan grits out between clenched teeth. His jaw is so tight, I'm worried he's going to crack a tooth, and his eyes flare red as his wrath demon comes out to play. For the most part, Nolan is pretty even-keeled, but when his demon gets riled, watch out. My toes tingle with the thought of him hate fucking me into submission. That will make up for missing out on the shower. *Oh yeah, baby, come to momma.* I eye the Taser sitting innocently on the bench. I wonder if I can load it and shoot him again, but then I think of a different way to really get him going.

Looking down at him, I shrug. "You scared me. I didn't think anyone was home." I refuse to apologize, knowing it will piss him off.

I know it worked when he growls and rolls onto his stomach, trying to lift himself up. Carter has stopped twitching too, but he just continues to groan. He's going to need to feed his lust demon to recover completely. I'm practically squirming with the thought of all the sex I'm going to get. I mean, it's not like they don't take care of me, because they really freaking do, but with my gluttony demon, combined with my latent lusty side, well, I just can't get enough.

Louis approaches me with his hands held out in front of him, like he is approaching a wounded animal. "Glory, pumpkin, what's with the Taser?" he asks, distracting me from my thoughts, and my eyes leave Nolan who is still trying to stand and move to my gluttony mate.

His chocolate brown eyes sparkle with laughter, but I can hear the concern in his voice. Ever since the kidnapping three weeks ago, the guys have been worrying about me nonstop. They have coddled the girls and me, and we've barely left the house except to take them to school and back, especially since they heard that Bridgette and her lawyer friend were let out on bail until their trial. I understand the girls, because what they went through was traumatic, but me? I've bounced back with no worries at all.

I shrug again, turning my back on Carter's and Nolan's struggles. "Nolan promised to take me to the shooting range and get me licensed to carry a gun so I could help with the bounty hunting business, but so far, nothing. You guys won't even let me leave the house to do my food blog. You're so worried about my safety, I bought myself some protection in the hopes that life can go back to normal."

A pair of hands land on my shoulders, making me flinch slightly, but the scent of my mate has me relaxing again as he puts one hand in my hair and yanks my head back, exposing my neck.

"Glory, did you just tase me?" Nolan growls in my ear and rakes his teeth along my neck, bringing goosebumps to the surface of my skin. My nipples pebble, and my core clenches. Oh yeah, there he is.

"Not on purpose, but yeah." I struggle a little—he likes it when I struggle. Sure enough, I feel his towel-covered cock start to harden. Damn, the man was just tasered with fifty thousand volts or whatever it is, and he gets up and gets it up like nothing ever happened. I have been truly blessed.

Louis snorts, so I think I must have said that out loud.

"Yes, Glory, that's right. You just zapped me with fifty thousand volts. What if I had been someone else, or even one of the girls?" Oh, I can hear how angry he is, and he makes a good point, but I just can't help myself.

"Well, Nolan, if you followed through on what you promised me, then maybe I wouldn't have bought it," I retort, trying to rile him further. I know I'm successful when his hand tightens in my hair and he bites down on my neck, but I'm not concerned, because I like a little pain with my pleasure.

"You know what happens now, don't you, Glory?" His words rumble over my skin as he releases my hair, only to grab hold of my waist and spin me before throwing me over his shoulder. His breathing is uneven in his anger, and he smacks my ass before moving toward the stairs.

"I'll just make some lunch for when you're done with her punishment," Louis calls.

Nolan doesn't respond, but I look up from where I'm hanging and shoot him a thumbs-up and a wink. He chuckles at my behavior as my eyes go to my last lover. Carter is watching me, and his beautiful blue eyes are filled with promise. I give him a little finger wave, and as he sits up, he mouths, "Soon," at me before he disappears from sight.

Nolan powers silently up the stairs. Every time I go to say something, he swipes a slap across my ass, eliciting a squeak from my mouth. Eventually, I give up and stay quiet until we get to wherever he is taking us.

We enter the bedroom the four of us share, and I expect him to throw me on our custom-made bed, so I'm shocked when he bypasses it and heads toward the walk-in closet.

He marches to a keypad on the back wall and starts pressing buttons. Now I always thought it was for a safe, so imagine my surprise when the wall of shoes pops open and Nolan walks through a secret door, closing it behind us. He flicks a light switch, and a gentle light illuminates the room as he puts me down on my feet and gives me a second to recover my equilibrium, but a second is all it really is. I don't even get a chance to look around the room before he drags me across it. He stops in the middle and reaches up to grab something. Dragging my hand up, he fastens my wrist into a cuff before doing the same with the other one, and then he steps back. Up until now, his big body has been in my way, but now that he's moved, I can see the room. Holy shit. It's a red room of pain.

I look at Nolan with delight and use a little more sass just to push him even further. "Shall I call you Mr. Grey?" My toes curl as I stand suspended before Nolan, whose eyes are still glowing red.

My mate's breathing is ragged as he stares at me. He doesn't make a move, he just waits, drawing out the anticipation. He's punishing me, and I can't wait to see what else he does. After five minutes of just listening to us breathe, the sexual tension building between us, he snaps his fingers and my clothes disappear

I'm naked, and the coolness of the room causes goosebumps to erupt across my flesh, but my nipples are tight and hard, and my core is dripping with desire. He steps out of my line of sight, and the room dims even more as he lowers the lighting. I'm nearly begging now, because the buildup is almost too much, but I know that's what he wants, so I grit my teeth.

A dark chuckle sounds as he steps up behind me. "Oh, Glory, you have more determination than I assumed. I thought for sure you would have caved by now and would be begging me." His breath whispers across my skin as he runs something hard down the line of my spine, and I shudder at the sensation before a sharp slap on my ass has me gasping at the shock of pain.

He moves to my front, and I see he's removed

the towel from around his waist, so my mate is gloriously naked. His sculpted muscles ripple with the tension that flows through his body as he runs the riding crop up the outside of my leg.

"What's your safe word, Glory?" he asks, his red, glowing eyes meeting mine.

"Macaron," I whisper as the crop makes it to the inside of my thigh, and the leather flap brushes across my sensitive folds.

Another dark chuckle leaves his mouth, and his lips curve up in a smirk. Whoa, Nolan is sexy as fuck. Who would have thought that he had a dom inside him? I can't believe this part of him hasn't come out to play before. We've been together for three weeks now, and this is the first time I'm seeing it.

"Good. Make sure if you use it, you mean it. Nod your head if you understand," he orders, and I do.

A cloth is wrapped around my eyes, blocking my vision, as he ties it tightly around my head. Now I'm bound and blindfolded and breathing heavily, and I can feel my desire start to dampen my thighs as my core throbs with need.

"You have been very naughty. Not only did you buy a Taser, you used it on your mate—on two mates, in fact. What do you have to say for yourself?" he demands, but I refuse to apologize.

"Nothing, I wanted protection," I retort, a wave of annoyance filling me, "and you weren't doing anything about it, so I took matters into my own hands."

Smack. The crop comes down across my mound just above my clit, and a squeal leaves my mouth.

"What kind of mates would we be if we couldn't look after you? Don't we take care of all your other needs, Glory?" The heat of his skin radiates off him as he steps closer to me. He pushes my hair back off my neck, and one of his hands circles it. "Doesn't Louis look after your gluttony demon with yummy treats, and don't we all take care of that greedy, gluttonous pussy?" He squeezes my throat just as he thrusts two fingers into my wet core.

A groan leaves my mouth, and my head hangs forward. I'm so fucking worked up. His fingers plunge in and out, and within moments, I'm on the edge of orgasm. Just as I'm about to tip over, he removes his digits, releases my neck, and steps away from me. The heat of his skin disappears, leaving my back cold.

"Uh-uh. Now that would be giving you a treat, wouldn't it? And we know you haven't been punished enough yet."

I'm so fucking needy, a sob leaves my mouth.

"Do you have something to say to your mate, Glory?"

I shake my head, unwilling to admit I might have made a mistake. He is kind of right. I was a little reckless by not reading the instructions before picking it up. I'm so glad the girls weren't here. "No."

Another smack comes down on my mound as I hear a click, and then a cold breeze touches my overheated skin as I hear someone else step into the room.

Nolan chuckles. "Oh dear, Glory. Carter's here, and he looks like he's starving now that he's used all his energy to recover from that ordeal. You're in some serious trouble."

This time, I feel a warm body step up to my front, and a hand slides into my hair before pulling my head backward.

"It's time to pay up, Glory," Carter whispers in my ear before his mouth comes down hard on mine. He bites my lip before plunging his tongue into my mouth and conquering it. It's all I can do to keep up with him before he abruptly pulls away. "On your knees. Now!"

There's a clanging sound, and then the restraints holding my arms loosen. Another sob escapes my mouth as they drop down. I'm unable to hold them up on my own, since they have become slightly numb. A hand presses on my shoulder, pushing me down, so I kneel, feeling a cushion under my knees as my arms are raised up until they are over my head again.

A little cry of pain leaves my mouth, but Carter's cock is against my lips, distracting me, and I feel precum weeping from it.

"Open up, Glory. I know how hungry you must be, so I'm giving you something to eat." His voice is all raspy, and he is panting. He must be starving too, so I stick my tongue out and run it along the length of his thick cock.

"Look at that, Carter. Isn't our mate so pretty on her knees? Now open wide and suck your mate's cock, Glory." Nolan's voice is close by as he gives his orders.

As I open my mouth wide, I hear the two of them kissing, and my mind envisions what it looks like as I take him deep into my mouth. He's long and thick, but being a gluttony demon has its benefits. My nose pushes against his pelvis as I swallow him down. Having no gag reflex is such a fucking turn-on.

One of them puts their hands in my hair and holds my head still, allowing Carter to fuck my mouth. He's not gentle either, and soon my eyes are streaming tears as he thrusts hard in and out. Breathing through my nose, I take everything he gives me. My pussy is now drenched, because I'm so fucking turned on. Suddenly, he pulls away, and silence engulfs the room again. The only sound I hear is my own ragged breathing as I try to recover from his punishing pace. Not knowing what's coming next or where they are is making me jumpy, but I know they would never hurt me, so it's also ramping up my anticipation.

I feel someone step in front of me again, and then a tinkling sound reaches my ears before I feel a mouth on each nipple. They bite and suck, and a groan leaves my mouth, my already tight peaks throbbing with sensation. I feel like I could come just from that stimulation alone, but it stops, and a sob of disappointment leaves my lips. I'm just about ready to beg when they clamp something on each nipple.

"Oh God." The pain is biting, but I breathe through it, and it starts to flow away. As it does, my mind begins to float.

"On your feet, Glory," Nolan demands. "It's

time you gave us what we want." Once again, I'm hoisted to my feet, my arms still above me. I open my mouth to beg them for what I need, but without any warning, I'm lifted, and as I wrap my legs around a hard body, I'm impaled on someone's cock.

"Fuck." A cry leaves my mouth as they force me down onto him.

"Yes, that's it, take it all," Carter rumbles as he forces his thick, long length into my core. "God, baby, you feel so fucking good."

Without giving me time to adjust, he fucks me like a madman, his cock pounding into my pulsing cunt as his mouth comes down on mine, his tongue mimicking what he's doing with his cock.

His hands move from my hips to my ass, and he gently parts my ass cheeks. Cold lubricant drips onto my skin before Nolan's fingers push in deep, stretching me none too gently. Another moan leaves my mouth, and Carter grunts.

"Oh, she likes that. She tightens so nicely when you do that." Nolan must decide he's stretched me enough, because I feel the blunt head of his cock at my entrance.

"Hold still for a second, will you?" he asks Carter, who stops his mad thrusts.

Pulling my cheeks wider, Carter holds me in place as Nolan's cock breaches my tight ring before sliding farther in.

"Oh my god!" My head falls back against

Nolan's shoulder as my eyes just about roll back in my head. All the sensations are almost too much, and my impending orgasm is just out of reach.

"Oh no, don't give up on us now, Glory," Nolan whispers in my ear.

He and Carter start to work in tandem, thrusting in and out of my body, using me as a vessel for their pleasure. No words are exchanged as the sounds of desire echo through the room—slaps of skin, grunts, and groans as well as heaving breaths. Nolan and Carter lean forward and exchange a kiss over my shoulder, and all I can do is hang on. They pull back, and suddenly I'm just about to tip over the peak.

"That's right, baby, come for us," Carter demands, and he pulls the clamps off my nipples.

The scream that leaves my mouth is nothing short of glass shattering as my orgasm explodes, sending shockwaves of delicious sensations through my body. The bite of pain makes the exquisiteness of the pleasure so much better, and through it all, the boys continue to thrust, but I can feel them struggle, and it's not long before they join me over the precipice. I feel their hot cum enter my body just as blackness surrounds me.

A tickling sensation down my spine wakes me a little later. I'm lying on my stomach in our bed, and I can tell by the dampness of my hair that they must have helped me shower before putting me to bed. I feel bodies on either side of me, and when I open my eyes, Carter is fast asleep next to me, so it must be Nolan on my other side. Turning my head, I watch Nolan's face as his fingers stroke gentle patterns across my back. My body feels relaxed, and his fingers are tickling my skin.

"You okay now?" I ask quietly, and when his piercing green eyes meet mine, I know he's back to normal.

"Yes, baby, I'm fine. It's been a while since we ran a bounty and, well, I guess I haven't been looking after myself like I need to." He blushes slightly and sounds a little ashamed, but I shake my head and turn so I can face him. His eyes drift to my breasts, but I put a finger under his chin and lift his eyes to mine.

"It's time to stop that shit now, Nolan," I tell him softly but firmly. "It's time for our lives to go back to normal. I want to see my parents and my sister. They have been patient up until now, but you don't want them to become impatient. I want to go out to eat. It's been lovely having you guys bring home different things, but I need to be able to experience the restaurants, not just the food, to be able to give an honest review. I also need the three of you to go back to life as normal. Neither you nor Carter have done any work for Wrathful Bail Bonds, Carter's club has been ignored, I haven't even seen it yet, and Louis's talents are missing at Tasty Treats."

He starts to argue, but I sit up, and my best weapons, my breasts, jiggle with the movement. Again, he gets distracted from what he was about to say.

"Not to mention you haven't done anything to get me trained for bounty hunting."

This gets his attention, and a frown crosses his brow as he sits up too. "Were you serious about that?"

An arm wraps across my waist, making me look over at Carter. I've obviously woken him, and I wince. "I'm sorry, I didn't mean to wake you."

Rolling over, he places a kiss against my back and shakes his head, his blond hair flopping down over his eyes. "No, baby, it's okay."

I give him a kiss, and his cornflower blue eyes heat. Carter needs more, but I have to finish this conversation with Nolan first. My annoyance flares at both his words and the fact that I'm hungry.

"Yes, I was fucking serious. I want in. I handled myself just fine when the girls and I were kidnapped. In fact, if I remember correctly, we had already escaped by the time you and the police arrived. I did that, no one else," I remind him, growling by the end of my rant.

"But, baby, there's nothing exciting or glamorous about it. It's not like TV shows or books. It's often boring and tedious, and we spend as much time doing paperwork as we do catching bail jumpers." He climbs out of bed, goes into the closet, and pulls on a pair of sweatpants before returning to the bedroom.

He throws one of his shirts at me, and I pull it over my head before crossing my arms. "I don't care. I need to feel useful and like I contribute to this family, but so far, I've brought nothing to the mating," I tell him, not wanting to meet his eyes.

"Oh, baby, no." He sits down on the bed and wraps his arms around me. "It doesn't matter to any of us, and you do bring something. You bring us together, and you bring much needed laughter and joy and softness into the house. You're giving both the girls and us exactly what we need."

My heart overflows with joy with his response, but I just can't shake the need to do this. Something is urging me, but I don't know how to explain this to him. Before I can try, though, Carter adds his two cents.

"If you really want to be involved, we can put you through the same training all our new bounty hunters complete."

My eyes shoot to his, and I see that he means

everything he's saying and he's not just trying to placate me. "Really?"

He stretches his arms over his head, and the muscles on his chest ripple, distracting me momentarily. "Yes, of course, but over the next six months, you will need to study hard. You don't just need to know how to take someone down. The courses involve intensive study in law, as well as skills training that include self-defense, firearms and nonlethal weapons training, and field training."

I pounce on his chest, unable to resist him any longer. "Oh yes, I promise I'll work and study hard." I rain kisses down all over his chest. "Thank you, thank you, thank you." His arms wrap around me, and I feel his cock harden beneath me.

Nolan chuckles behind me, smacking my ass as he stands up. "Alright, I'll go get that organized. You'll start with the next class, which is next week. How about you look after Carter, because I'm pretty sure he still needs something." He winks and heads into our closet to get dressed.

Carter turns my face toward his and takes my lips, showing me how hungry he really is for the next few hours.

By the time Carter is finished with me, it's late afternoon. When I come downstairs, I find the girls in the kitchen with Louis and Nolan, eating a snack Louis put together for them.

"Mom!" Zoe shouts and tries to climb down off the chair she's sitting on, but I beat her to it.

I place a huge kiss on her cheek before tickling her. "Zoe bear, I missed you so much," I tell her over her giggles.

"Daddy said you were a bad girl and that Uncle Carter was giving you a time out in your room," Zoe says as I put her back down.

Looking at Nolan, I raise an eyebrow, but he just shrugs with a smirk.

"What did you do? Did you try to flush a Barbie down the toilet?"

"No, Zoe, I didn't flush a Barbie down the toilet." I snort at her question before moving to Aria who is looking at me with worried eyes. "Are you okay?" I ask Aria, and she gives me a shaky smile before throwing her arms around me, hugging my waist tightly.

"Yes, but you can't be doing naughty things,

Mom. I don't want Daddy to be mad at you. I don't want you to go away."

My heart melts at her words. Her mother's abandonment really had an impact on Aria. My eyes drift to Nolan for help, because I'm not quite sure what to say.

He has a worried frown as he steps toward us and picks Aria up, hugging her tight. "Baby, you know Bridgette leaving wasn't anyone's fault but her own, don't you? Nothing you or I did was responsible for that, and Glory isn't going to leave just because she got into trouble, but she did something she shouldn't have." He puts her back on her chair, and his gaze moves between the two girls. "It's just like if you and Zoe touch things you've been asked to leave alone or don't ask permission for. Glory is an adult, and she should know better."

"Yes, I got into trouble, but Daddy is right. I did something that was silly and dangerous and put other people at risk. I didn't think, and I deserved to be punished." In fact, they can punish me anytime, but I don't tell the girls that. "But that's not going to make me leave. Nothing will make me leave you guys ever."

"Promise?" Aria looks at me, her bottom lip quivering. Oh God, the poor girl. I wish I hit Bridgette harder in the face with that shovel.

"Yes, baby, I pinkie promise." I hold my finger out to her, and she grabs hold of it with hers, a wide smile crossing her mouth. I guess a pinkie promise is just as sacred now to a five-year-old as it was when I was five.

"Alright, now that that's taken care of, how about I get you a snack?" Louis asks, coming up behind me and giving me a kiss on the cheek. "You must be starving, you missed lunch."

Zoe gasps. "Uncle Carter made you miss lunch? You must have been very bad."

Just then, Carter joins us, giving both girls kisses before helping himself to a beer out of the fridge.

"Yes, Zoe, Glory was very bad, and both Daddy and I had to punish her."

I roll my eyes at the innuendo, thankful that it goes over the kids' heads.

"Well, let's not talk about that anymore." I change the subject before Zoe asks any more questions. I'm not sure how I could explain to them what I did.

Before anyone else can speak, the doorbell rings.

Nolan looks at me. "Are you expecting any more packages?"

I shake my head. "No, nothing. What about you guys?"

"No, we had nothing planned today." Louis frowns.

I head to the front door, wondering who could be there. When I open it, my heart leaps into my throat.

"Surprise!" my mom shouts, looking thrilled to be here.

Standing behind her are two of my dads, my brothers, and my sister, Serena. They are all holding an assortment of gifts and balloons. Movement behind them has me peering over their shoulders. Standing on the driveway is my other dad, and in his hand is a lead rope attached to a pony—a freaking pony.

I'm still speechless when my mom pushes her way past me. The scent of her perfume is a familiar, comforting smell from my childhood, and her blonde hair is perfectly styled, but my mom is always perfectly styled.

"I just couldn't wait anymore. I know you all have been recovering from such a harrowing ordeal, but it's not right for a granny not to be able to see her grandbabies."

Not quite sure what to do, I wave for the others to come in and hurry after the main source of trouble. My mother had no problems finding the kitchen, and when I walk in, she's bundled the girls into her arms and is smothering them with kisses, leaving bright pink lipstick all over their faces. My mates look a little shocked at the whirlwind that is before them. Once done with the girls, my mom moves onto them. One by one, she smacks kisses on their lips, and all three of them are too surprised to do anything as I watch with a smirk on my lips. Of course my lust demon mother would go for the lips, son-in-laws or not.

Taking a deep breath, I step into the fray. "How

about we move into the living area where there's enough room for all of us, and I can introduce you all there?" I suggest, and Nolan looks at me with panic.

"There's more?" he asks, and I can't hide the grin that crosses my mouth. My big wrath demon is scared of my hurricane mom.

"Yep, looks like you're about to get a crash course in the Luxure family ways," I tell him before hurrying after my mom who has already grabbed both girls by the hand and dragged them with her. They initially looked a little worried, but by the time I get to the living room, they are all giggles and laughter as my family smothers them with gifts and love.

"That's French for lust," Louis says quietly behind me as we watch the chaos in front of us.

"Yup, Mom's family originated in France, and my dads all took her last name, which is tradition in a family with more than one husband."

I turn to smirk at the three of them. "Which means you're going to all end up as Luxures too." I wave my engagement ring at them, a little worried that they might not want that, but they all beam with happiness.

The sound of wrapping paper ripping and the girls' delighted squeals have me turning back to watch the chaos.

My mother, Petra, is looking at the girls with tears of joy in her eyes. She knows all about what happened with their mother and couldn't believe someone could be so cruel to their own flesh and blood. She promised me there and then that the girls would never want for anything.

"Glory, what do you want Nicholas to do with the pony?" my father Duncan asks. He's standing near the front window, gesturing outside to where I guess Dad still is.

"A pony?" Nolan's question comes out strained.

"Yes, every princess should have a pretty pony," my mom announces without even looking away from the girls.

"Is she serious?" Carter asks, sounding just as strained as Nolan.

"Yup! Both Serena and I had ponies almost as soon as we could walk. Mom is old school, and she believes everyone needs a well-rounded education. The things that we know how to do would astound you," I reply as I move farther into the room. I can feel them follow behind me and decide I should make some introductions.

"Can he just load it back onto however you got it here for now? You may have to take it back home with you, and the girls can go there for lessons," I tell my father, and he nods, his shaggy blond hair bouncing with the movement. His blue eyes, which are so much like mine, roll at my words.

"I said the same thing to your mother, but she insisted we bring it so they could see it." My gluttony demon father walks past me, giving me a kiss on the cheek before opening the front door and shouting, "Just put it back in the truck for now, Nic. It has plenty of hay to eat." I don't hear what my greed dad says in response, but Duncan gives him a thumbs-up and closes the door again.

"Dad, come sit down so I can introduce you all," I tell him as I take a seat on the couch next to Valen, my sloth demon father, whose half-lidded brown eyes tell me he's almost asleep on the comfortable furniture despite the chaos surrounding him.

He gives me a drowsy smile when I kiss him on the cheek. "Introduce us, Glory, while we wait for Nic to deal with the animal."

Nolan, Carter, and Louis have all moved into the room, and Zoe gets up from the floor before running over to her dad with a box in hand. "Look, Daddy, Grammy got me my very own cell phone." She shoves the box into his hands, and he opens it for her, making all the right impressed sounds. It's a toy phone, because my mom is not ridiculous enough to give a three-year-old a real one. Well, actually, she probably would if she knew I wouldn't yell at her.

"Carter, Louis, Nolan, Aria, and Zoe." I point to each individual as I say their names. "This is my family. You all know Serena." She waves but doesn't say anything from her spot on the ground, where she helps the girls by gathering up all the wrapping paper.

I step around her and Aria, moving to my mother and greeting her with a kiss on the cheek and a whisper. "You could have called first." Louder, I address everyone else. "My mother, Petra, my fathers Duncan and Valen, and my brothers Silas, Seth, Callen, and Kade." I gesture to each one as I say their names. Everyone exchanges greetings and polite niceties. "And my father Nicholas is the one wrangling the pony." I gesture outside.

The balloons that my teenage brothers were holding are now sitting on the ceiling, and they are all watching the girls with patient smiles on their faces with an occasional eye roll for our mother. My brothers are two sets of twins. Callen and Kade are nineteen and greed demons, and Seth and Silas are eighteen and sloth demons. Luckily my mom had so many husbands to help, because she was very busy for a few years there. There are only about ten months between both sets of twins. This is probably the last place they want to be on a Friday afternoon, but we're a close family, and they have been sending me constant text messages about wanting to meet my mates, especially when they found out that Nolan ran a bounty hunting business and Carter a club.

Random chatter is exchanged while Louis and I put together a spread of coffee and cakes that he just happened to bake this morning. God, I love being mated to a chef and fellow gluttony demon. He just gets me on a whole other level.

Once seated, I make sure everyone has something before sitting back and watching my family with a kind of joy I've never felt before. Smiling, I watch as Callen and Kade grill Nolan about being a bounty hunter. It wouldn't surprise me in the least if they tried to wrangle an invite to the academy. They have been adrift since they graduated, and nothing has caught their interest. I'm pretty sure they have slept their way through the female population of their age range. Maybe they should be asking Serena for a job instead. Man whores at nineteen, Mother should be so proud. Well, she probably is proud of them, seeing as she's a lust demon.

The girls are having a tea party with a little china set that was another gift that Mom gave them. The three of them are sitting around the coffee table, and Mom is giving them a proper lesson on how to pour tea—another one of my mother's ideas about well-rounded education. Her mantra used to be: "You'll thank me one day, just you wait."

The little cups and saucers tinkle as the girls use shaky hands to pick them up. Tea sloshes over the side, but it's mainly milk, so it won't burn them if some does escape the saucer.

A feeling of contentment washes over me as I watch my family, new and old, socialize. I take a sip of my own coffee just as the front door opens and my father Nicholas walks in.

"The pony is all happy in the truck, munching

on some hay. I told you they would have no place to keep it," he says, aiming the last little comment at my mother who rolls her eyes.

"Yes, dear, you were right," she placates him as he comes over and places a kiss on my head.

"Hiyah, princess." He then introduces himself to my mates before helping himself to a rather large plate of cakes and pastries.

"Really, Dad?" I ask, and he just shrugs.

"Wrangling a pony is hungry work." Not to mention the greedy man can't help himself.

"Tell us a little bit about yourselves," my mom prompts now that everyone is fed and watered. "I mean, demon matings happen instantly and so suddenly, but usually there's a period of adjustment before people move in together, yet here you all are, living together within days. I know Glory's dads and I would feel better if we knew you all a little better."

The room is silent as my mother's words sink in, and then Serena and my brothers explode into laughter.

"Really, Mom, you're going to try to pretend to be a somewhat normal parent? That was very human of you. I bet you've been practicing that speech since you found out Glory met them," Serena teases, and my fathers chuckle as my mom blushes a pretty pink.

"Well, she's the first one of you to meet her mates. I felt like it was necessary to make sure she is going to be looked after."

"There isn't much you can do about it, love. It's fate, after all." Duncan pats her on the shoulder as the laughter fades.

"Not to mention we didn't even wait a day to move in, and I'm pretty sure you were pregnant within the first month." Valen smirks on the sofa as all of us grimace with the thought of what the four of them got up to in that first month.

"Eww, okay, change of subject." Serena waves her hands around. Lust demon or not, no one wants to hear about their parents and sex. "So I hear Carter owns a club. The boys were just saying that they need jobs now that they have just finished school. Both sets do. The lazy bums can't sit around on their asses for the rest of their lives. What about giving them something to do there?"

The conversation moves on to a safer topic, though the guys still react weirdly when Serena suggests giving Seth and Silas jobs. The boys look interested in the prospect, which in itself is a miracle, since getting sloth demons to be enthusiastic about anything is difficult, but my guys quickly change the subject, and that makes alarm bells ring instantly. I tuck that little bit of information away to bring up at another time. I want to know what they are hiding. Secrets won't work in this family. Mated or not, I will not put up with them hiding shit. There is a way of breaking a demon mating, and I wouldn't hesitate to use it if I thought this was a mistake.

The following Monday after my family descended upon us, I am up early and wearing a pair of stretchy cargo pants with a Wrathful Bail Bonds trainee shirt that Nolan gave me the night before. My body is humming with excitement, something that has been missing from my life for a while now.

Sure, I loved my food blog and life was pretty good, but I just felt like I was in a holding pattern and going through the motions. Since I met and mated the guys, and now have the girls in my life, I feel so much more… fulfilled, like it was meant to be, which I guess is how it all works really. Now, though, the thought of doing more is exciting.

I saw the guys' faces when I asked to do this and the doubt and disbelief in their eyes. Was I hurt? Maybe a little, but then again we really don't know each other all that well. They don't know that as a part of my well-rounded education, I went to many different martial arts classes with Serena. Mom advocated for her daughters to be able to defend themselves in any kind of situation, and between my three dads, they decided we needed to know how to fire a gun as well, which then led to other kinds of weapons training as the three of them got a little carried away. The defensive driving classes also came in handy occasionally, so to say that I think the boys are going to be surprised is an understatement. They are not wrong about me needing training in law, since I don't have a clue about any of that, but I am so going to nail the practical skills.

I know when they look at me, they see a curvy, fun food addict, but there's more to me than people see, and I love being underestimated. It's how I was able to beat the kidnappers and Bridgette. My brain works in such a way that it's able to calculate all the possible scenarios. If I hadn't been so unstable after the mating with the guys, I would have been able to conjure a gun and capture the kidnappers, but I'd been so worried about the girls that everything I knew kind of left my mind momentarily, and that was how they were able to get us into the van. I also didn't want the girls to get hurt in the crossfire, so I played possum and let them take us.

It all worked out in the end, thankfully, and now that our mating has stabilized, I don't think I'll ever have any power problems again.

Placing a cup under the coffee machine, I press the button, and while it does its thing, I make the girls' lunches. Once that's done, I get the fixings for omelets out of the fridge and start to chop up some veggies to go in them. The smell of coffee must drift through the house, because Louis stumbles into the room shirtless, his dark brown hair in disarray. A smile crosses my lips at the sight. Louis is always so together and refined, a product of his French childhood, and seeing him mussed is sexy as fuck.

He worked late last night, so he must have slept in his bedroom instead of climbing in with the rest of us.

"Good morning, sugar plum." He leans in and gives me a sleepy kiss on the head before moving straight to the coffee cup.

Not happy with that, I grab him by the back of his pajama pants and haul him backwards toward me. A yelp of surprise leaves his mouth as he stumbles, but he quickly rights himself and turns to frown at me.

"Oh no, none of that grumpy shit." I point at his wrinkled forehead. "You need to give your mate some morning sugar since she missed out last night."

His frown disappears, and a smirk crosses his lush mouth. Grabbing me around the waist, he pulls me close so our bodies are pressed together, and my nipples pebble with the contact. I run my hands up his naked back, feeling his muscles ripple as I trail my fingers across them.

"What was I thinking? Will you ever forgive me, my *dulce leche*?" He leans in and nibbles on my neck, his stubble tickling me.

"Hmm, sweet milk, I'll let you taste my sweet milk," I taunt as his soft lips press against mine in a gentle contrast to the way his hard cock grinds against me.

A growl comes out of his mouth as his hand drops to my thigh to wrap it around his waist. "I'll gladly drink your milk."

"Milk! I'll have some milk please," Zoe announces as she walks into the kitchen, already dressed and ready for playgroup. She drops her backpack on the ground and climbs up onto one of the stools.

Louis groans in frustration but places another kiss on my lips before he drops my leg and adjusts himself in his pants, his back to Zoe.

"Can it be chocolate milk, please?" she asks, blinking her eyes owlishly, a new move she thinks makes her look sweet and innocent.

"Not for breakfast, Zoe," Aria tells her as she catches the question. She is also dressed, looking adorable in her private school uniform.

"Aria's right, Zoe, plain milk for breakfast, or there is juice," I tell her, and a big smile crosses Aria's face while Zoe sticks her tongue out at her.

The two girls are polar opposites of each other. Zoe is lively, loud, and sassy whereas Aria is quiet and introverted and tends to flinch if I raise my voice, even if I'm just laughing. I cried the first time it happened, but Nolan assured me it's nothing I've done and that Aria was subjected to more of Bridgette's torment and nasty ways. We've discussed getting some therapy for her, but we're going to wait and see if having a positive female influence around her makes a difference.

I grab the girls a bowl of cereal each, and they eat it quietly while Louis and I drink our coffee and I prepare us both an omelet.

"Where's Daddy?" Zoe asks through a mouthful of cereal as I whisk the eggs.

"He went into work early this morning because he has a new training group starting. I think Carter went with him, and then he's going over to his club to do some things." I turn to Louis. "You know you've all been very secretive about that club. Is there something I should know about, or is there something the three of you are hiding? Every time I ask about it or ask to see it, you all change the subject."

Louis frowns, his eyes still a little foggy with sleep. He looks between me and the girls and shrugs. "Nothing we've been hiding really. He hasn't been in since we met you, and his manager does a great job of running it." He once again avoids the question.

Putting down the bowl of eggs, I cut up some onion and mushrooms, the knife flying across the board with my agitation. The girls and Louis watch in fascination as I dice and chop like a master.

"Wow, Mom, you're really good with that knife, but aren't the veggies small enough now?" Aria says, and when I look up, her eyes are clouded with worry.

My gaze drops to the veggies, and I realize I've annihilated them. In my annoyance, I didn't pay attention, and now there is nothing but tiny, itty-bitty pieces of onion and mushroom. I slam the knife down and plaster a smile on my face.

"Whoops, ha-ha. Oh well, I guess they will still be alright in the omelet." I notice that the girls are finished. "Why don't you both run upstairs and brush your teeth, and then we will do your hair and I'll drop you off on the way to my first day."

They both jump down from their stools and run back upstairs. I hear them arguing on the way up the stairs. Once they are out of earshot, I whirl on Louis, holding my knife up in a threatening way.

"Right, you have one chance to tell me what the three of you are hiding. I won't tolerate you concealing shit from me. I am not a damsel in distress, nor do I need you to protect my delicate sensibilities or whatever shit you imagine you may be doing. What the fuck are you hiding about Carter's club? When my brothers asked about it the other day, you all looked uncomfortable. Carter said he didn't think it was a good idea that they worked there. What's up with that?"

Louis runs a hand through his messy hair and blows out a breath before he mutters, "I told those assholes we should have been upfront with you. I knew you wouldn't care." He looks up, his chocolaty caramel eyes meeting mine. "It's a sex club, Glory, and Carter is the dungeon master." He looks like he's waiting for me to blow up.

"And?"

"What do you mean, and?" he asks.

"Well, he's a lust demon and was unmated, so what's the big deal about that? Serena runs a brothel. Why would I judge him for that? You need to feed where you can when you're unmated."

His mouth drops open in surprise, and he stutters a bit before I stop him.

"Are you trying to tell me that you guys thought I was going to be upset with that?" He nods, still speechless. "Pshh, what a load of shit. You guys are idiots. As for my brothers working there, I don't care, and they won't care. Remember, we have lust demons for a mother and sister. Plus, they have their own latent tendencies. It might be good for them, especially for Seth and Silas, who won't need to sleep as much if they are able to side feed." Turning on the stove, I pour the eggs in and finish making the omelets, while Louis watches me like I'm about to explode at any second.

"You really don't care?" he asks quietly, and I whirl to face him.

"Is he still going to be sexing women up or whatever it is a dungeon master does?" I ask, pointing the spatula at him. He vehemently shakes his head. "And is he going to take me there to have some fun?" This time, he nods slowly. "Then why would I get upset? It's his place of business. I'm just bummed I haven't had a chance to check it out, though I was looking forward to shaking my ass on a dance floor. I thought it was that kind of club."

"Oh, it is one of those too," he assures me as I slide his finished omelet toward him and place mine next to his on the table.

Turning off the stove, I go around and sit next to him, placing a kiss on his cheek. "Well, that sounds even better. Eat up and go back to bed, you look like crap."

He is kind of stunned again, so I roll my eyes. They really must have had shitty girlfriends in the past if they are walking on eggshells around me, but I don't have time to ease his worries, so I scarf down my omelet and finish my coffee. When the girls return, I quickly put their hair up into braids and hurry them out the door.

Their chatter during the drive is a great distraction for the nerves that are now plaguing my stomach. I'm excited about the new opportunity, but stepping out of your comfort zone is always tricky no matter how confident you are. I just hope I don't embarrass the guys. They are letting me join the class on a pure leap of faith. They have no clue what I can do, and for that, I love them even more. Now I just have to try my hardest to make that leap of faith be the best thing they have ever done.

Chapter Five

Wrathful Bail Bonds runs bounty hunting classes twice a year but rarely has the opportunity to employ any of the people who take it due to their low staff turnover. Their students are often in high demand, however, because of the high caliber of the graduates, so none of them stay unemployed very long.

The classroom on the second floor of the Wrathful Bail Bonds building is noisy when I walk in, but it soon descends into utter silence as everyone turns to look at the newcomer. As I scan my fellow students, I realize there are three times as many males as there are females, and two of the three females there give me the same look of disdain I experienced when I first went to Tasty Treats before I met my guys.

Well, I'm not here to make friends, so I ignore them and my eyes go to the third girl. She gives me a shy smile and a nod, and as I step into the room and head in her direction, I hear the first sly shot from one of the males. Of course they couldn't just keep their mouths shut. Nope, he decided to judge me on my looks alone and not what I could do.

"Hey, honey, I think the receptionists work downstairs."

Seriously, the dude must be a few sandwiches short of a picnic. I mean, I'm wearing the same thing as him and everyone else in the room.

I met the receptionist downstairs. I wanted to check out who was working with my mate after the disaster at Louis's workplace. The older, matronly woman introduced herself as Stella and gave me a big hug, welcoming me to the family. She had been so excited to meet Nolan's new partner, and she gave me my ID card and showed me where to go. She was kind, but I could tell she has a spine of steel. Nolan informed me that she was the mother of one of his bondsmen. She lost her husband and had been lonely. When Nolan heard that, he offered her a job, and she's been his receptionist and general Wonder Woman for the last three years.

Turning, I eye the dude up and down. He may be judging me by my looks, but I am totally going to do the same. I know when he looks at me, he sees a curvier than mainstream acceptable brunette, who possibly doesn't look like she's fit enough to take down a fleeing criminal, but I worked hard to keep a balance between my curves and being fit. He might find me lacking, but I have all I need to succeed in this job.

"I can assure you that I am most definitely in the right spot. Are you sure you are?" I look him up and down. "Steroid Abuse Anonymous is actually in a different building."

His face blazes red, and he balls his hands into fists, taking a step toward me. Whoa, someone has anger issues. That was a quick reaction, even if I was taunting him. Before anything can happen, though, Nolan walks into the room.

"Right, grab a seat. We have a lot to get through over the next few weeks to make sure you're ready and able to take on being bail bondsmen."

"And women," one of the girls titters, and I roll my eyes. I think I'd rather worry about whether I can stop a dangerous criminal than whether they call me by the correct gender.

Nolan, ever courteous, smiles. "Of course, and women."

The girl flutters her eyelashes, and I grit my teeth.

Wrathful Bail Bonds is not a demon exclusive agency, and many of the people who train are humans, so being a demon is not taken into consideration. To pass the exam at the end, I can't use any demon enhancements to get by. It also means that I asked the guys to keep our relationship on the down-low. Nolan and Carter both wanted to argue the point, but I don't want anyone saying I got in by nepotism or whatever, even if I did—not to mention the judgment that usually comes along with multi-partner relationships—but seeing her openly flirt with my mate makes me want to cut a bitch.

Everyone takes seats at the individual tables. I got one in the middle of the group, right next to the girl who smiled at me before. Putting my bag under my chair, I pull out a pen and a notebook. I'm going old school, because I want to make sure I get everything I need to know.

"Welcome! For those who don't know me, I'm Nolan Zorn, and I'm the co-owner of Wrathful Bail Bonds. For the next six weeks, we are going to run you through every possible thing you will need to know to be the best you can be, and when you leave here, you will have all the skills necessary to catch even the sneakiest of criminals."

The room buzzes with first day excitement.

"I'm warning you now, most of it is boring, tedious work, so if you think you're going to be some big action hero chasing down bad guys, think again. There are computer checks and running down leads, talking to witnesses, and basically chasing your own tail. Only a small percentage of this work is physical." He looks at most of the guys when he says this, and a couple of them squirm under his scrutiny. "There's a first aid component, as well as a tactical component. Surveillance, interrogation, and apprehension will also be covered."

I watch as he paces back and forth in front of the classroom, my mind going to everything hidden by his uniform, and I lick my lips. Concentrating may be a bit of an issue if he's going to be all commanding and shit.

"To be considered for this class, you all indicated that you are proficient in some form of self-defense. You will be tested on your abilities. We will also work with weapons, knives, guns, and Tasers specifically, but the biggest thing we will be going over is all the rules and regulations we must follow, and all the legal and ethical issues a bounty hunter must adhere to. You only have to mess one thing up, and then you become the one in trouble with the law."

There's some murmuring around the group, but everyone is mostly hooked on his words.

"One of the things you will be doing is the leg work for some current cases we have. If you do it well, and we're happy with your performance, we will take you along when we go out to apprehend the perpetrator."

The murmurs get louder at this announcement, and I can practically feel the excitement in the air.

"But first things first, a history of bounty hunting." Nolan puts a PowerPoint presentation up on the interactive whiteboard for us to go over, but before he can start his lecture, a hand flies into the air from that same annoying female.

"Aren't you going to call roll?" she asks with a tilt of her head.

"I'm assuming if you're here, this is where you are meant to be. If anyone is missing, they are either late and have no respect for me, or they are stupid and they have no place being a bounty hunter," Nolan drawls, and she flushes. "But I guess we can do a quick introduction around the room and get it out of the way. How about you go first?"

She quickly jumps to her feet and smooths out her T-shirt, which fits tighter than mine or any of the other women's.

"I'm Bobbi-Jean Jessop, and I want to follow in my daddy's footsteps. He has a bounty hunting business in Shreveport, Louisiana, and is one of the best bounty hunters out there. I think it's such an honorable thing, helping law enforcement when they aren't able to do the job."

Nolan is nodding. I know that nod—it's the one he gives the girls when they are telling him some inane thing and he wants them to think he's paying attention when he's probably replaying some hockey play he saw last night in his head.

"Right, okay. Is that Bobby John Jessop's company? Hard Ass Bonds?" Oh look, he was paying attention. Will wonders never cease?

She preens at his attention and nods her head. "You've heard of him? Well, he is pretty well known in these circles."

"Well known for something, alright," Nolan mutters under his breath at levels humans can't hear, but I do. There's a story there, one I plan on finding out. "Thanks, Bobbi-Jean." He gestures for her to sit.

"Oh, it's BJ," she tells him before sitting down.

The rest of the class snickers like a bunch of twelve-year-old boys. Oh come on, it's funny.

Everyone else gets a chance to introduce themselves. The dude who gave me a hard time when I first came in is a police academy washout, though he words it in a way that makes him seem like it wasn't his fault. Nolan's brow creases at this information. He obviously wasn't aware of this when he approved this guy for the course. That shows a lack of background checks. I wonder how it slipped through. I guess he has been very busy the last couple of weeks, what with our mating and the kidnapping and all the sex… Lots of sex. It's no wonder his brain hasn't leaked out of his ears.

Eventually, it's my turn. Standing up, I look around at the rest of the class.

"Hi, I'm Glory. I was a food blogger and social media influencer, and now I'm looking at trying something different, a new challenge in my life, and I'm really excited about it."

Most people are polite, smiling and nodding, but the two who have been assholes since the moment I walked in mutter under their breaths, and of course, I can hear them.

"You can tell with that ass," BJ sneers cattily, and roid boy, whose name is Jeff, says, "I'd like to influence that ass."

A thunderous look crosses Nolan's face as I sit down, ignoring them. It's really no skin off my nose.

People like that are just assholes, and nothing I can say or do will change that, but I can see my wrathful mate is ready to lash out, so I pipe up.

"I'm really excited to hear all about the history of bounty hunting, sir." That last word changes the wrath to lust, and his gaze swings to mine with so much heat, I feel like I might spontaneously combust. It's brief, because he remembers where we are, but it gets him back on track.

For the next three hours, we talk about bounty hunting history and tradition. Lunchtime rolls around, and we are all dismissed. He points the way to the lunchroom and advises on what's available nearby. The rest of the class filters out, but I remain seated, writing down the last of my notes. Once the last person exits the room, I use my powers to close and lock the door before getting up and walking to the front of the classroom. Nolan is sitting at his desk, his Wrathful Bail Bonds shirt stretched deliciously across his chest, and his hair is mussed because he spent all morning running his hand through it as he lectured.

He leans back in his chair as I approach, a warm smile on his face. "Excuse me, sir, but I have a question regarding the lecture."

His smile turns into a smirk, and his eyes sparkle with amusement. "Oh yeah? What exactly did you want to ask?"

I trail my finger along his desk as I move around

to his side. He swivels his chair around to face me, his legs spread slightly.

"I was wondering if using seduction is an acceptable way to apprehend a fugitive?" I run my finger up and down his pant leg while I flutter my eyelashes and bite my lip.

"I'm not sure, Ms. Luxure. I would need a demonstration of the technique to really be able to tell you if it was acceptable or not."

"Oh, should I find someone to help us?" I tease, and a growl escapes his mouth while a snort of laughter escapes mine. "Maybe you'd be willing to play the role of the fugitive?"

"I'm sure I can manage to sacrifice for the cause."

I kneel between his legs and reach up to pull his zipper down. He shuffles a little lower in his chair and grunts.

"That is certainly getting right to the point." His erection springs from his pants, thick and long and mouthwatering.

I run my tongue along the length before swallowing it down. His musky taste floods my tongue as I wrap my hand around the base and bob up and down on his shaft.

Nolan moans and slips his hands into my hair. "Oh yeah, I would surrender immediately with this kind of incentive."

Lifting my head, I giggle. "I better be the only apprehension agent you're surrendering to… or

Carter. Oh, maybe we can do role play at home. Bounty hunter and fugitive. We can take turns being the fugitive."

I put my mouth back on his cock, and he groans even louder, using my hair to give himself the pleasure he's chasing. A tingle flows through my body, and I feel my panties grow damp with desire. The knowledge that I'm able to please my mate is a huge rush, not to mention the naughty scenario.

He increases his thrusts, and his cock hits the back of my throat, causing me to choke slightly, but we both moan with delight. I love it when they are a little rough. Using my hands, I cup his balls and roll them, feeling them tighten as he gets closer to the finish.

"Yes, Glory, don't stop," he murmurs quietly as he thrusts one more time, filling my mouth with his cum, which I quickly swallow down.

Easing back, I lick his length and clean him up while it still pulses in my hand.

When he stops, I tuck him into his pants and lean back on my heels, looking up at my satisfied mate. "So?" I ask him sassily.

His eyes widen, and he grabs hold of my hair, yanking me onto his lap. "If you ever use that technique on anyone else, I will kill them without question," he growls before kissing me hard.

I purr at his alpha behavior. His hand slips into my panties, but before he can get anywhere, the door rattles like someone is trying to get in.

"Damn it," I complain as we both look at the door. I can see shadows on the other side through the frosted glass.

The door rattles again, and with a sigh, Nolan removes his hand and lifts me off his lap and onto my feet.

I narrow my eyes at the door. I may very well kill whoever's on the other side.

Chapter Six

The simpering, southern tones of BJ come through the door. "Nolan, I was wondering if I could talk to you a little more about the history of bounty hunting."

A growl escapes my lips, and Nolan snorts. "Well, you were the one who wanted to keep our relationship quiet. Say the word, and I'll shout it out for everyone to hear." He stands up and places a kiss on my cheek. "Do you think I like it when people ogle my mate's ass?" He moves me around to the other side of the desk while I'm still fuming before sitting back at his desk and waving his hand to unlock the door. "Come in."

"It's locked," she calls back.

"Try again, it sticks sometimes, but it's not locked," he replies, and sure enough, she gives it a hard push and comes barreling into the room.

When she rights herself, she looks from me to Nolan, her eyes narrowing in suspicion.

"Glory was just asking me the same thing," he tells her, but it doesn't seem to ease her suspicion. So she's not so stupid after all, I guess.

"Thanks so much, Nolan, I appreciate your extra attention on this," I say, standing up. "I'll just let you go over it with Bobbi-Jean, and I'll go and get some lunch."

"Okay, but don't be late back. My business partner will be in this afternoon, and he gets annoyed at tardiness. He likes to dole out punishments for infractions." His words are full of innuendos that thankfully go over BJ's head, but I squirm at the thought of Carter punishing me again. Sign me up.

"Punishments?" she asks with wide-eyed innocence, and he startles. I guess he forgot she was in the room. That's good for my ego at least.

"Ah, yeah, you know push-ups and shit. He's a stickler for rules and regulations," Nolan answers, trying to backtrack.

Gathering up my things, I wave goodbye and leave him to suffer through her inane questions and deliberate attempts to flirt. I'm mostly secure in my relationship with my guys, and food is all that is on my mind now that I know an orgasm is out of the question.

When I make my way downstairs, Stella is sitting at her computer, and she smiles at me when she looks up. "Hello, dear, how was your first morning?"

I lean against the receptionist's desk. "It was really interesting. I had no idea that bounty hunting started in the Middle Ages, and it's fascinating that instead of money being put up, a person put themselves up as collateral. I'm not sure there's anyone I would have risked being hung if they escaped." Well, a few someones, but that goes without saying.

"Nolan and Carter are so thorough in what they teach. It's no wonder that our graduates always find jobs not long after they finish." She sounds proud, like a mother, and that makes me wonder about my guys' families.

Waving a distracted goodbye, I head outside in search of some lunch. I'd seen a taco truck that looked promising when I arrived, and now I have a craving for Mexican street food. Setting off down the street on foot, I ponder if any of them mentioned their families before. I know we haven't been together long, and all the drama involving Bridgette and the fallout from that has overshadowed things, but apart from Nolan's sister, Bella, I have no clue if any of them have any. A wave of guilt rushes over me. I've been so self-involved, I haven't thought about asking either. They were kind enough to put up with all of mine, so the least I could do is find out about theirs. I make a note to ask them over dinner tonight and show them that I have an interest in more than just what their dicks can do for me, which is a hell of a lot, to be honest.

A smile crosses my face at the thought of their dicks and them using said dicks on me or each other —I'm not fussy.

"Well, I've never seen someone smile like that

before they have eaten my food." The slightly accented voice has me looking up at the interior of the food truck. I didn't even pay attention to what was on the menu, because my mind was so distracted by dicks. An older Latino woman is smiling at me with a twinkle in her eye.

I blush a little at being caught daydreaming about dicks but shrug. "If you had been thinking about what I was thinking about, you probably would be smiling like that too."

She chuckles. "I don't doubt it, *chica*. Now, what can I get you to eat?" The smells coming from her truck are amazing, and my stomach rumbles with joy.

"I'll take five tacos, surprise me with a mix of fillings, and a bottle of sparkling mineral water please." I think about my poor mate back at the office who's missing out on lunch. "Actually, make it twelve and two waters."

The lady goes about preparing my order, whistling while she does, and I check my messages on my phone. Mom has sent me one wishing me luck today, and Callen and Kade have both sent me one asking me to hook them up with the next round of classes. I reply to them, saying I'll see what I can do. I don't see the harm in them working for Nolan, and I'm pretty sure if I asked nicely, he'd give my brothers jobs. If he's stubborn, I'll just have to get back down on my knees and beg. God, I hope he's stubborn.

I pay the lady, gather up my big order, and walk back to the office. When I get there, I stick my head back into the classroom where BJ is still monopolizing an increasingly frustrated Nolan.

"Nolan, Stella asked me to bring your lunch to you when she found out I was going to the food truck to get mine."

He jumps to his feet, relief in his eyes. "Bobbi-Jean, I hope you don't mind, but I need to grab myself something to eat before classes resume for the afternoon."

Her face drops slightly, but she shakes her head. "No, not at all. I've enjoyed our conversation, and please, call me BJ."

He runs a hand through his hair. "Ah, yeah, sure, BJ." The poor bastard looks so uncomfortable calling her that, I chuckle to myself.

"Glory, if you could just bring it to my office, that would be great," he tells me, exiting the class-room and leading the way. The look BJ throws me once his back is turned is pure evil, but I just smile politely and follow my mate.

"I can't wait until it's time to work on self-defense," I say to Nolan as he gets to a closed door and pushes it open, allowing me to enter. He follows behind me and clears off his desk so I have some-where to put the food.

"Why self-defense?"

"So I have a legitimate reason to kick that girl's ass."

He chuckles, running his hand through his hair once more. "Glory, you're a goddess. I'm starving, and I don't think I could have listened to her a single minute longer. She was talking about her father and all the reprehensible things he's done to catch criminals. So many of them are illegal." He's frowning, and I can tell he's having a moral dilemma.

"Let it go, babe. He will get his comeuppance eventually. Someone will call him out on his practices, and he will have to shape up or lose his license."

I hand him his seven tacos and his water, and a groan leaves his mouth as he bites into the first one. "God, I love you."

It's my turn to chuckle now. "I'll see you later," I tell him, taking my food and preparing to leave.

He stops eating and looks up with a frown. "Where are you going?"

"To eat my lunch in the lunchroom with the rest of the class. It already seems suspicious that BJ caught us in your room with the door closed."

He rolls his eyes. "Who cares? Carter and I don't. Just tell everyone, and then I can eat lunch with you or close my office door and bend you over my desk like I want to."

Phew, I fan my face with a napkin. I am so tempted to say screw lunch since we were interrupted before, but I'm starving, and I also want to get a feel for my class. Not that we're competing against one another, but I would still like to know who I'm going to be up against when it comes to showing our self-defense skills.

"Can't. Sorry, babe, but I need to do reconnaissance, check out the competition, and get the lay of the land," I tell him, and he narrows his eyes on me, but I just blow him a kiss and head back the way I came.

Back in the lunchroom, the groups are chatting loudly, but everyone stops speaking as I walk in.

BJ whispers behind her hand in a highschooler kind of way to the girl sitting next to her, then I guess she gets some balls. "How come you were bringing lunch to Nolan? And why were you in the room with him earlier with the doors closed?"

Is she fucking serious? "I'm sorry. I'm not sure what makes any of that your business, and we're not in high school, so it really wouldn't matter if I was in there on my knees giving him a blow job, would it?"

Her face screws up with indignation, but the rest of the group just laughs it off and goes on with their conversations. Nobody else gives a crap, nor do they think that what I said was the truth. Silly fuckers.

The girl who smiled at me earlier is sitting apart from everyone else, but she waves me over and gestures to the seat next to her.

"Thanks, ah, Kerry, wasn't it?" I take the seat next to the pretty, dark-haired girl I sat next to in the classroom. She took as many notes as I did.

"Yes, and you're Glory, right?" Her voice is quiet with a slight accent I can't quite figure out, but she has exotic features too, so I'm guessing her origins are not American. Maybe some kind of Latin American heritage.

I nod as I take a big bite of my taco, knowing our lunch break is almost over and I have to hurry if I want to make sure I don't demon out in the afternoon. "Sorry, I'm starving, and hangry me is not a good idea," I joke, but I see her look down at my hand where my demon mark is before she nods. Ah, okay, so I guess she's not human. I hadn't thought to look for fellow demons in the class. Humans can't actually see our marks, only other demons can.

I keep eating my food, but my eyes drop to her hands now, looking for her own mark. Sure enough, there's the mark of a greed demon.

"Oh hey, you're a…" I trail off, not wanting to say it out loud in case someone is listening. She smiles and nods. "So what got you interested in bounty hunting?"

"Well, like BJ, my dad has his own bounty hunting business, but he exclusively hunts demons. His agency is basically Lucifer's law enforcement, and when you do something wrong, there's no bail or human jail or anything like that. You get dragged back to Hell for your punishment, and that's his company job. Both my brother and I work for him, but my brother is a sloth demon and not really suitable for takedowns. He prefers to do all the research from the comfort of his desk and gaming chair, so that leaves me, and Dad wants me to be trained by the best, and Nolan and Carter are exactly that. Lucifer has been asking them to join his squad for ages, but they would have to be based in Hell, and they couldn't move there because Nolan's kids still had contact with their mother."

Holy shit, that's another thing I just learned about my mates. Maybe I should stop jumping their bones and actually have some deep, meaningful conversations with them. Now that Bridgette isn't in the picture, perhaps they will want to take Lucifer up on his offer.

"I've been training for it my whole life, but he wants me to have a license I can flash around on Earth. Most of his other hunters have done the training here as well to cover our asses if we need to deal with law enforcement."

"Holy shit, BJ would crap her pants if she knew you were going to work for Lucifer." I chuckle at the thought.

She laughs with me before nodding down at the mark on my hand. "I couldn't help but notice that you have mate circles, and, well, they look to be the same as our distinguished lecturer," she pries, changing the subject.

"Yup, Nolan, Carter, and their friend Louis. All mine." I'm smug, but I have every right to be, because they are a real catch.

Her eyes widen. "Wow, the holy trinity is off the market. I bet the general demon population doesn't know this yet, otherwise there would have been an uproar."

I feel my brow crease in confusion, and I stop inhaling my food. "What do you mean?"

"I don't recognize you, so your family must not have spent a lot of time in Hell, but the majority of the demon population spends a lot of time going back and forth from the Earth plane to Hell, and it's a bit like a who's who of the demon world. Those three are some of the most eligible demon bachelors around. The fact that they are a throuple as well is just the icing on that beefcake. Female demons everywhere are going to be pissed."

I look at her warily. "But you're not?"

She screws up her face. "Fuck no. Nolan's sister was my best friend growing up, but we lost contact when she moved earthside. My brother was one of his best friends, but they had a falling out about something. I'm not sure what, but Nolan's like a brother to me, and he often stays with me if he has to come to Hell for any reason."

Well, okay then, something else I just learned about my mate. I'm feeling more than a little guilty now, and I decide to steer the subject away from me and my mates.

"So tell me, what's Lucifer like? Have you met him?" I'm super curious about the demon leader. Mom and the dads respect the hell out of him, but they also like living on Earth. They said Hell was a cesspool of gossip and intrigue. I guess that's why I've never been.

Kerry blushes at my question before clearing her throat. "Ah, yeah. We lived in the palace when I was growing up. Mom and Dad still live there, and once I join Lucifer's enforcement crew, I will have to move back, but at the moment, I'm enjoying being on Earth. Having my own apartment, away from watchful eyes, has been a blessing."

"And what's he like? I hear he and his three lieutenants are scary powerful."

She shivers, and I'm not sure if it's from fear or desire, but when she meets my eyes, hers are carefully blank.

"They are scary and seductive, and when you're in their presence, it's hard to work out which way is up."

Whoa, sounds like there might be a story there, but Kerry stands and balls up her trash. "Come on, let's get going, we're going to be late."

Okay then, I understand not wanting to talk about something, so I let it go, but when I get to know her better, I'm totally grilling her about this. I might have to set up lunch with Bella. I'd like to get to know her better as well, and I'd be reuniting old friends.

Happy with my plan, I finish the last of my tacos and get to my feet. Excitement about the afternoon's session thrums through my body.

"Let's do this."

Chapter Seven

Once lunch is over, we all head back to the classroom we were in this morning. Standing in front beside Nolan is my sexy lust mate. I can practically hear the girls sigh at the sight of him, and possibly a couple of the guys. There's just something about him that screams sex.

"You're all late," he barks as everyone sits down in their seats.

"What, a whole two minutes?" Jeff scoffs, and I watch as Carter's gaze zeros in on him.

Wow, gone is the sexy, flirty man and in his place is a tough, no-nonsense disciplinarian. I can definitely see the dungeon master now, and a shiver runs up my spine, but I don't think Jeff squirms because of the same reason. Carter's eyes seem to glow slightly as he raises an eyebrow.

"Two minutes can make all the difference between catching your mark and him getting away," he growls.

I roll my eyes internally, thinking maybe he's taking this a bit far, but hey, he's the boss.

He starts to stroll around the room, his hands behind his back, looming over everyone in their seats. "This afternoon, we will assess your self-defense skills before moving on to laws and regulations tomorrow morning. You will eventually be tested on these, so I suggest you take detailed notes. Anyone who doesn't get a ninety or above will not receive their bounty hunting qualifications from us."

A murmur runs through the class, but nobody says anything.

"Right, I will be handing out a book that outlines laws and regulations for bounty hunters in each of the American states. Don't think you can get away with learning only the laws of the state you plan to work in. Sometimes, you will be required to retrieve a mark from out of state, and you'll need to know the laws of that state as well. Each morning, we'll go over state laws, and in the afternoon, we'll be working on more practical skills. These won't be limited to self-defense and weapons training, but they will give you the skills you need to do the leg work involved with chasing an escaped criminal down. We will also test your people skills as well as your computer skills, but for now, let's hand out the booklet and then we'll head downstairs to the gym."

The murmuring of the group gets louder as he drops a stack of books on each table in the first row. "Take one and pass them back. Once you have yours, you can head downstairs and get changed into suitable workout gear. We're going to see what you can all do."

A wave of excitement thrums through my body, and I wait patiently for the books to reach me. Grabbing one, I pass the rest behind me then stand up and throw my bag over my shoulder. Side by side, Kerry and I head downstairs to change. I'm in the process of pulling my shirt over my head, leaving me in just a sports crop top, when BJ and the other woman in our class walk into the changing room.

"Don't think I don't know what you're doing," she sneers at me as I unzip my pants and shimmy out of them, leaving me in just panties and the crop top.

I roll my eyes. I'm not in the mood for confrontation, so I don't engage.

I pull on a pair of yoga pants and tie my hair back into a ponytail, leaving my feet bare. I'm ready to go, but I wait for my new friend.

"You don't have a chance with him. He's bounty hunting royalty, and so am I. We're meant to be, so I suggest you stay away from Nolan if you know what's good for you."

I see Kerry smirk out of the corner of my eye, but I still don't engage with her delusions as much as I'm dying to.

"You may want to leave your engagement ring in your bag," Kerry suggests casually as she ties her dark hair into a ponytail as well.

I can practically feel BJ's and her sidekick's gazes zoom in on my beautiful engagement ring. I'm reluctant to remove it from my finger, but she's right. I don't want to damage it in any way during sparring or hurt anyone with it.

Sliding it off my finger, I tuck it into the coin part of my purse, which is in my backpack. It should be safe there.

"Okay, let's go."

We leave the other two and make our way into the gym. It has the typical smell of sweat and disinfectant and is filled with the unmistakable sounds of male grunts.

The guys in our class obviously changed quicker than we did because they are all working out on some of the equipment. Two are using treadmills, while a few of the others are lifting weights. I can see Nolan in a corner talking to another one.

"Ladies." Carter's gravelly voice has us turning toward it.

Holy shit. My mate is fucking fine. He's wearing a pair of loose-fitting shorts and a tank that is showing off all his delicious muscles. I lick my lips, and Carter's blue eyes zero in on them, and then a slight smirk crosses his mouth before he becomes Captain Hardass again. "Grab a treadmill and warm up while we wait for the last two."

Kerry and I do as instructed, and once the other two ladies join us, Carter starts the session. "You can spend thirty minutes warming up, stretching, or doing whatever you need to. Over the next six weeks, we will be testing everyone's cardio fitness, which will require one-on-one time with Nolan and me while you run on the treadmill. I suggest if you're not as fit as you hoped that you spend time out of class working on that."

Oh yeah, I know exactly what I can do to increase my cardio fitness, and I squirm just from thinking about it. *Fuck no, Glory, we said less sex, more talking.* Damn it, I may have to start taking Max for a run.

"After that, we're going to spar in short three-minute rounds. Winner will advance to the next round. It will be a good way for us to judge your strengths and weaknesses."

BJ's hand shoots up in the air, and she waves it around, but Carter ignores it.

"And yes, you will be fighting the opposite sex. You are not guaranteed to have a same-sex bounty, so you need to know how to deal with marks that are bigger or smaller than you, and how to restrain them without hurting yourself or them in the process. Right, get to it."

Her hand drops, and a look of disappointment settles on her face, but she and her friend, whose name I can't remember, take the last two treadmills.

For the next fifteen minutes, I warm my muscles up before hopping off and stretching. I think everyone is antsy to start, because before long, we're all standing around, waiting. Down at the far end of the gym is an area set up for sparring, and Nolan and Carter wave us over there.

They don't waste any time, and the matches are fast and furious for the first three rounds. The guys obviously feel like they need to prove something. The winner changes a couple of times, and Jeff is the latest winner.

Nolan and Carter exchange a concerned glance before Carter calls out, "Glory, you're up." I tamp down on the urge to smirk. I know the guys are concerned, but here's my chance to get my own payback for that comment this morning.

"Are you sure? I don't want to be responsible for hurting a chick." Jeff chuckles, looking toward the rest of the guys for support, but they are all quiet.

He beat a couple quite badly, and I guess the others aren't idiots, so he gets no response. We're not using pads, and he went hard. Although head shots are not allowed, he managed to give one of them a bloody nose with a stray elbow.

Nolan and Carter look at me, trying to keep their expressions neutral, but I can see their worry.

"It's fine, I'll just do the best I can," I tell them, and I hear BJ and her friend titter behind me.

"Alright then. You guys know the rules, no head shots. Winner is decided by Nolan and me." Carter gives his instructions and passes me a pair of boxing gloves, which I pull on.

I bounce up and down on the spot just to warm my muscles up again, then I climb into the ring.

Shuffling into the middle, I hold out my gloves so I can bang them together with his. He gives me the briefest tap and then he's on me. I stumble backward, trying to get my guard up and shifting my body to the side, and when his punch lands, it glances off my shoulder. I narrow my eyes. *So it's going to be like that, is it?*

He smirks at me as he bounces around on his toes. Idiot! All he's going to do is wear himself out, but that works for me. He feints and jabs a couple of times, but I don't engage. I wait him out, so then he starts talking trash.

"Don't be scared, just throw a little punch so they can see you shouldn't be in here, and then I'll finish the fight. You shouldn't lie about your abilities to get places, it's dangerous." The condescending ass chuckles.

He throws another punch, and I block it, but the strength behind it rattles my bones. Fuck, he's not holding back. I wait him out, trying to get a feel for his fighting style and not wanting to show my cards too soon.

He throws another couple of jabs and an upper-cut, and as I lift my guard to protect my face, I make the mistake of leaving my chest open, and he lands a punch right on my left boob. A woosh of air escapes my chest as the pain barrels through me, and I stumble back a little bit, tears welling in my eyes.

I hear shouting behind me, but I can't turn

away from the asshole in front of me. He's smirking like he already won the fight, and he drops his guard slightly. It's just the opening I was looking for. Dropping my shoulder, I spin and kick out, hitting him in the head and knocking him the fuck out. He crashes to the ground with a thud, and the room is deathly silent except for my breathing before everyone erupts into noise. Most of the other people in the group are cheering, but I can see one or two are complaining about my head shot.

When I look at my mates, they are glancing between me and the idiot on the ground in disbelief. I pull off my gloves and drop them onto the ground before cradling my boob. I don't care what people say, that shit hurts.

Nolan and Carter quickly climb into the ring. Nolan goes to Jeff, checking to make sure he's still alive. I may have put a little bit of demon strength behind the kick, but I didn't hear his neck crack, so I think he'll be okay. Carter rushes over to me.

"Shit, are you okay?" He grabs my arms and goes to pull me against his chest, but I hold firm.

"Stop it," I whisper. "You're going to make them suspicious."

He looks up at the rest of the group watching us and grits his teeth, growling quietly so only I can hear.

"I'm fine." I shake off his worry and his hands, then I bend down to pick my gloves up. "I'm ready to go again."

Nolan stands up. "Ah, I think we're done for the day. Can someone call the paramedics? We should get Jeff looked at."

Carter steps away from me after I give him a little nod and pulls out his cell.

The class is dismissed after that. When I'm heading back to the changing rooms, I get a couple of pats on the back from some of the other guys, but when the changing room door closes behind me, BJ is on the attack.

"What did you do that for, Glory? Couldn't stand that you were losing so you went for an illegal move?" She looks me up and down. "That's just sad. That's not going to impress Nolan or Carter if that's what you were hoping to achieve." She turns around, leaving me stunned and fuming.

"Did you not see that tit punch? How legal was that? At least I didn't retaliate with a nut shot," I growl at her, fisting my hands at my sides so I don't actually strangle her. That's frowned upon for humans apparently. "I'm looking forward to our match, BJ."

She freezes at that last comment, but Kerry grabs me and hauls me back over to my gear.

"Settle, Rocky, you'll get your chance. Just make sure you keep it clean so she can't call foul."

Fuming, I get changed out of my gear and back into my street clothes. I don't shower, I just want to get out of here. I'll have one when I get home. I'm so frustrated with myself. I allowed him to get to me, and my demon rage got the better of me. Maybe I need to eat a little more for lunch to keep that under control in the afternoon.

Grabbing my bag, I wave goodbye to Kerry and tell her I'll see her tomorrow, then head out, ignoring the other two women in the room. When I get out to the reception area, I stop suddenly at the sight. Leaning against the reception desk, chatting with Stella, is Louis.

He spots me and stands up straight, a brilliant smile crossing his face. "There you are, my little dumpling," he croons, his French accent thick as he holds his arms out to me. "I hear you've had a rough afternoon, and I am here to whisk you away."

I cross over to him and sink into his embrace, breathing in his unique scent, and my world is right once more. I shudder from the relief his hold brings me. He kisses the top of my head, and I can hear him talking to Stella, but I'm not paying attention. Maybe I'm having mate withdrawals. I mean, we haven't been together all that long, so perhaps a whole day of no touch was just too much.

I hear the door open behind us and voices spill out, but they stop abruptly. I pull away and turn in Louis's arms. Kerry is smiling widely, but BJ and her friend Samantha, whose name I finally remember, are staring wide-eyed at Louis. Stepping back, I look at my mate, and I can completely understand the stares. He's wearing a light gray suit that fits him like it was made for him, which it probably was, and his green tie brings out the chocolate brown of his eyes, making them sparkle.

He stiffens slightly at the scrutiny, and he must feel my own shaky emotions, because he waves a hand at Stella. "We must be going. I want to take my beautiful fiancée out for dinner before we head home. I want to celebrate her greatness in this newfound career." His French accent gets thicker, and he's really laying on the charm.

Stella just giggles and waves her hand at the two of us. "Get out of here, you rascal."

"Who's that?" I hear Samantha ask BJ, but I don't hear her response as he whisks me out the door and into a sleek, low to the ground sports car.

"Wow, I've never seen this one before," I tell him, running my hand across the smooth, buttery leather seats.

"It's no good as a family vehicle, so I only take it when I don't need car seats," he explains as the car roars to life. He reaches over and grabs my hand, raising it to his mouth and placing a kiss on my palm. "Come on, my little demon. Let's feed you and you can tell me all about it. Then we will go home, and *la petites filles* will smother you with love and all will be right with the world. Then, I will smother you with some more love and life will be even better." He winks, his eyes sparkling with heat, and I wriggle at the thought of the kind of love he will be smothering me with.

Maybe we can skip the rest and get straight to that.

"Oh no, *ma belle*, food first, the rest can wait." He starts the car with a push of a button and the engine roars to life, then he pulls out of the parking lot.

"What about my car?" I ask him as we pass it, and he waves a hand.

"Leave it, it will be safe, and you can get it tomorrow."

With that reassurance, I grab my engagement ring out of my purse and slip it onto my finger. Sinking back against the leather seats, I ignore the dull ache in my chest as I look forward to whatever Louis has planned.

The next few weeks are hard. The laws are tricky and vary from state to state, and we're required to know them all. I spend most nights going back over them, trying to memorize them, and fall into bed each night exhausted. The practical side of the course is just as intense. Jeff was fine, and after a day or two of rest, he was back to normal, but Nolan and Carter haven't allowed any of us to spar one another again, so I still haven't had my chance to beat down BJ, who continues to flirt with my mates.

We've been going through old Wrathful Bail Bonds cases, which all contain detailed notes on everything they needed to do to find the bond skip. Most of them are straight forward legwork, calling around, talking to family members, finding out where they liked to hang out, and casing those places. Some of them involved more creative measures.

After this week, where we will be doing weapons training, we will actually get to work on active cases, shadowing some of the bond agents to see what they do. We're to observe from the car, but I'm still excited to see some action. I hope I get assigned to Nolan.

Carter has had to work at his club the last week, so I haven't seen him as much. I'm hoping to change that this weekend too. I'm going to visit him at the club as a surprise. He's been working so hard, trying to find someone to replace him on a more regular basis, but so far, no luck. Louis says he actually has a couple of good prospects training with him at the moment, so things should be getting better soon. When he has to work at his club, he stays at an apartment above it, not returning home. I know he can get energy from the club, but I'm worried he's not getting enough, so I'm going to top him up while I'm there. I can't wait.

I'm meeting Kerry and Bella for a girls' night of drinking and dancing beforehand, though, and I'm excited for that too.

The gun range is silent as I arrive in the morning, but I'm pretty sure that's going to change soon. I'm running a little late because Zoe had a meltdown over her hair, and it took me a while to sort out.

I'm out of breath as I rush into the classroom area of the range. Everyone's eyes turn to me as the door bangs closed behind me.

"You're late," Carter barks, and Nolan is also looking at me with a frown.

Hang on now, assholes, I was dealing with your daughters. I stop and cross my arms and tap my foot. "I'm sorry, my daughter had a tantrum about her hair, and it took me a little while to get it fixed." I raise one eyebrow at them, and they both lose their frowns very quickly.

"Right then, family comes first," Carter says awkwardly and waves to a chair. "Take a seat. We were just going over the standard gun we use here at Wrathful Bail Bonds."

I slide into a chair next to Kerry who is smirking at me, knowing I just smacked the guys down even if nobody else does. "Everything okay?" she whispers, and I quickly nod and murmur, "Yup, just a semi-normal day in our household."

"Okay, listen up. You've been learning all about the rules and regulations a fugitive recovery agent must follow, so you know that carrying a gun differs from state to state. It is your responsibility to check these laws before arming yourself or risk being arrested. You will also need a permit to carry a weapon in whichever state you are entering, so that's another thing you can't forget. Many states prohibit FR agents from using excessive force and carrying weapons while apprehending a fugitive, and you can and will be arrested on a weapons violation, so educate yourselves, people."

Nolan is leaning against a desk with his arms crossed over his chest, his Wrathful Bail Bonds shirt stretching tightly across his biceps. God, I wonder if I can corner him somewhere later. I haven't had sex with any of my mates in weeks. Carter hasn't been coming home, and I've barely seen Nolan except when I stumble into bed after a long night of studying. Louis is always home in the mornings, but then I'm busy getting the girls ready for their day. I'm feeling lonely and deprived and getting a little desperate.

"So while we cover guns during this course, whether or not you can carry will depend on each individual company you work for. Our agents tend to stick with Tasers, since there's less chance of accidentally shooting the wrong person with them, but we do carry guns in cases of fugitives with a history of carrying their own weapons." Carter picks a gun and magazine off the table in front of him. "We prefer to use the Glock 19 when we do use one, and that is what you will be using today." He slides the magazine into the gun, making sure the safety is on before placing it back on the table. "We will also go over loading your magazine and cleaning your weapon." His gaze lasers in on Jeff. "Don't roll your eyes at me. Gun maintenance is an important part of owning and using a gun, and I want you to show me that you can do it. You don't like it? There's the door. Don't let it hit your ass on the way out."

Nolan moves away from the desk, goes over to a cabinet, and pulls out a familiar item. When he turns around, he's looking at me, and there's a wicked glint in his eye. "The weapon we carry and use the most is the Taser, and today, we will also be using them on each other."

The room erupts into protests as the rest of the class argues against this practice, but I just raise an eyebrow at my smirking mate. I see how it is. I guess I won't be trying to corner him after all. I have plenty of toys to take care of my sexual frustration.

"Silence!" Carter roars. "It's good to know the firsthand effect it has on someone's body, and it's also good to know when a Taser possibly won't work. Can any one answer that question?"

Quite a few hands rise, and Carter points to Kerry.

"Tasers not working can be attributed to a few things." She counts off on her fingers. "One, it could be missing one or both probes. Two, the perpetrator's clothing might be too loose or too thick. Three, the cartridge might be faulty. Four, drug use, and five, excessive movement."

"That's correct. Thanks, Kerry." Carter smiles at my friend, and the other two girls give her dirty looks, which makes me chuckle quietly. "There are also a few lucky people who just won't be affected by it. You need to be aware of this and be prepared in case this occasion arises. I have a sheet you can all grab when you leave on Taser statistics. When they are effective, they are great, but if you deploy one and it fails, all you're going to do is succeed in pissing the victim off more, and then the situation will escalate. Though not the most ideal of solutions, they are still better than reaching for a gun every time, and it's what we recommend."

Huh, I didn't think about what might happen if the Taser actually failed to subdue someone.

"Let's all hope that none of you get in that situation, but it's also why we like to have a dog on our team," Nolan says, going over to the door and opening it.

Max bounds in and circles the room, his nose to the ground as he sniffs, until he stops in front of my bag. He sits down and barks once.

Carter comes over and picks my bag up, patting Max on the head. "Good boy, Max."

I narrow my eyes at my mates as he digs around in my backpack before pulling out weed.

"Holy shit, does that mean she's expelled from the class?" BJ sounds excited, and if looks could kill, she would be dead at my feet.

Nolan chuckles and calls Max to the front. "No, we planted that in her bag before she left yesterday, and it's not illegal in our state anyway. Max isn't just good for sniffing out drugs, which is not his primary job, though it does come in handy sometimes. He can also bring a suspect down with less chance of being injured than a human. You will all be suiting up and learning how this feels today as well, so how about we get started? We have got a lot to get through."

"Put your gear on the shelves in the back of the classroom, then go to the gun vault where Carter will issue you a weapon and safety gear. Please speak up if you need some help with anything."

I see BJ and Samantha exchange a conspiring look, and then their hands shoot into the air. "We will need some help," BJ calls.

Carter narrows his eyes on them. "You were supposed to have basic weapons experience to get into this course."

The girls pale a little, and BJ backtracks. "Oh, we have, but a little refresher wouldn't hurt." It's not like they can deny it unless they want to risk being asked to leave.

Once everyone has been handed an unloaded gun, a magazine, and a box of ammunition, they are sent back to their desks. For the next hour, we go over loading a gun, breaking it down, and cleaning it. Once Nolan and Carter are satisfied with everyone's skills, we're led to the firing range to take out a few paper zombie targets.

I sit out of the way, the noise and ear protection making it a little tricky to have a conversation with Kerry who's sitting with me. Max, who has been left to roam until it's his turn to work, sidles up next to me and flops down at my feet, drooling contentedly on my boots. I let everyone make use of the three lanes, in no hurry to prove anything to anyone. I watch as everybody uses their two allotted clips, comparing shots and talking trash, so I don't notice when bitch boy sidles up next to me. I swear he just likes the sound of his own voice, and

I can't believe he's still trying to get a rise out of me.

"I noticed you haven't had a turn yet, Glory." There's no need for him to lower his voice over the sound of everyone firing their guns. In fact, he raises it a little so I can hear him with my earmuffs on. Idiot. I see Carter and Nolan swing their heads around to watch. The dumbass doesn't know about our advanced hearing and thinks nobody will notice over the sound of the gunfire.

"Maybe she doesn't actually know how to. I did see her coming out of Nolan's office the first day. Maybe she was performing special favors to get an easy pass on everything." BJ steps up next to him, the two of them obviously trying to catch me out in something. "I wonder what her fiancé would think if he knew."

Huh, well, she's not wrong about the special favors, but only because it was fun and not because it got me anything. And, well, she's not really one to throw stones in glass houses. Both of my mates have reported her offering them special favors for a guaranteed pass.

I'm done with these two bitches. Standing up, I put my safety glasses on before slamming the magazine into my Glock 19 and shoving the other one into the back pocket of my jeans. I step up to an empty lane, pull the used target forward, and then clip up a new one before running it down to the end. Taking my preferred stance, I sight up the bullseye. Breathing in and out, I pull the trigger, carefully putting five of the fifteen rounds into the target. All five hit the zombie's brain directly.

Taking one hand off the gun, I hit the switch and push the target farther back. I put five rounds into the zombie's chest before sending the target back again. This time, I put the last five rounds through one eye, each bullet hitting in exactly the same spot. Once my gun empties, I place the safety back on and set it down on the bench before bringing the target forward. Taking it off the clips, I spin to discover a crowd has gathered. Nolan and Carter look surprised but impressed, but it's BJ's and Jeff's faces that make me the happiest. I hand the target to BJ before going over to Nolan.

"Well, boss, what did you think of that? Did I really need to give you a blow job on the first day to pass this course?" With that, I grab hold of his hair and pull his mouth down onto mine, kissing him hard. Next, I pull away from him and do the same to Carter before turning back to a stunned BJ. "And as for my fiancé, he'd want to know why he wasn't invited."

With that mic drop, I pick up my empty gun and make my way back to the storage locker, my head held high. I was a little sick of all the flirting anyway. Now I've staked my claim, and they can fuck right off. I think I just proved that I have the skills to do what needs to be done. I just hope I pass the theory side of it too.

I hear footsteps behind me, and when I stop and look, both Nolan and Carter are there.

"But... But... But you told us you didn't know how to use a gun," Carter stammers, still looking shell-shocked.

I'm not sure if it's my gun skills or my kiss, because he's rocking quite the hard-on behind his pants.

"You kept asking me to take you to the gun range, begging me to teach you to shoot."

I wink at him and smile. "A girl has to have some secrets, and if you had, then I probably would have pretended not to know what I was doing just for you, but this is Wesley Snipes serious, and I wasn't pretending to fluff your egos."

I leave my two mates and continue on to the changing rooms. I'm starving and horny. I wonder if I drop in and see Louis on the way home if he will take care of my needs. I'm pretty sure that's a no-brainer.

Chapter Nine

"Thank fuck it's the weekend," I grumble as I collapse into one of the comfy sofas in the living room. It's late again, and both girls have eaten dinner and had baths and are now watching something on TV that involves puppies and firetrucks or police cars or something.

The girls turn and look at me with their mouths wide open. "Mom, you said a bad word!" Zoe exclaims, and Aria narrows her eyes at me.

"The F-word requires five dollars in the swear jar."

I lean my head back against the cushions. Damn it, I'm so tired, and I hadn't even thought before I opened my mouth. "You're right, I'm sorry. I will do that as soon as I can get up," I tell them without opening my eyes.

I've been working hard for the last month without a break. I come home, cook, clean, and then study. I'm exhausted.

I've decided I'm taking the whole weekend off. I'm going to sleep in and do something with the girls during the day, and then I'm heading out with the older girls Saturday night. Sunday, I plan on sleeping off a hangover.

I'm drifting off to sleep when I feel two small bodies climb onto the couch on either side of me and snuggle in. I open my eyes and smile at my beautiful girls.

"Hey, this is nice," I tell them, wrapping my arms around each of them and snuggling them into my side.

"We've missed you, Mom," Aria says while Zoe just cuddles.

"I know, I've missed you both too," I murmur. "How about we do something together tomorrow? What would you like to do?"

They both start to rapidly throw ideas at me, and I hold up my hands, laughing. "Slow down, you can each choose something. Aria, you're the oldest, so you can pick first."

"I'd like to get some boots and pants for riding the pony at Grandma's place." Aria shyly looks up at me from under her eyelashes. I'm so proud of her for asking for what she wants. The poor little thing is finally starting to come out of her shell from all of Bridgette's horrible treatment.

"I think that sounds awesome. I can't wait." I look down at the sassy little cherub who's just about busting a gut, waiting for her turn. "Okay, firecracker, what do you want to do?" I wait on tenterhooks for whatever crazy idea she has.

She bats her eyelashes at me, wearing an innocent smile on her face. "I'd like to go to Build-a-Bear, and then to Tasty Treats for dessert with Louis."

Well, hey, that's not too bad. Aria's shaking her head furiously at me, but I just ignore her.

"Yeah, that sounds like fun. I can't wait."

"What sounds like fun?" Louis comes in and sits on the couch, moving a giggling Zoe so that she's on his other side before lifting my feet up into his lap. Pulling my shoes and socks off, he presses his thumb into the arch of my foot, and I groan in relief.

"Mom's going to take us to Build-a-Bear," Zoe replies, leaning against him, and he stops rubbing and looks at me in horror.

"No!" he gasps, and I shrug.

"What? It's just building a stuffed bear, it's no big deal, and then we're going to have dessert at Tasty Treats."

"I will have the whiskey ready for your teapot," he assures me with a shudder before turning to the girls. "Well, if you're having adventures tomorrow, you best go to bed and get a good night's rest. Go and brush your teeth, and after I've given Glory some food, I'll come up and read you a story."

Zoe whoops, throws herself across Louis, and wraps her little arms around me, planting a kiss on my cheek before scrambling down and racing upstairs. Aria is slower but does the same thing and follows at a more sedate pace.

Louis stands and puts my feet down on the couch. Leaning down, he gives me a kiss on the head. "Stay here. I'll bring food to you, and then once I've read the girls a story, I'll run you a bath."

"You are my favorite mate ever. That deserves a bathtub blow job if you'll hop in with me."

His eyes light up. "Right, one very short bedtime story for the girls coming up." He hurries off to the kitchen, and I chuckle as I stretch out, closing my eyes. The TV is still playing in the background, and I hear, "No problem is too big, no pup is too small," as I sink into oblivion, but before I can really fall asleep, a wet tongue on my cheek has me squealing and sitting up.

Max's tongue is hanging out like he's laughing at me as I narrow my eyes on him. "Not cool, dude."

Max has become my new favorite ever since he took BJ down during our lesson on attack dogs. Oh my god, I laughed so hard, I swear a little bit of pee escaped. She screamed her head off as he dragged her around on the ground in that huge protection suit that made us look like sumo wrestlers. It helped that when he got to me, he wouldn't attack.

After I outed our relationship that day with the guns, there were a few grumbles from BJ and Jeff, but that soon stopped when they realized we didn't care, and Nolan and Carter weren't going to get rid of me. Apparently, Nolan received an irate call from BJ's father, but after Nolan asked if he would prefer to pull his daughter out instead, he shut up. I've more than proven I belong on the course and that I have the skills needed to be a fugitive apprehension agent.

Another heavy sigh escapes before I can stop it, and Max leans his head on my thigh, his unusual eyes staring at me in hope. "You're waiting for my food to arrive, aren't you?" I ask him dryly, and of course he doesn't answer me, but I know the truth.

"Here, babe, sit up and have this, and then you can relax. I was thinking instead of a bath, why don't we pull the lid off the hot tub and sit in that?" Louis suggests as he hands me a steaming bowl of his delicious beef bourguignon. It's a thick, rich French casserole with lots of beef and carrots, and it's yummy and just the thing I need after a long, draining week.

I sit up quickly, taking the bowl from him. "What a freaking amazing idea! I'd forgotten we had it."

He goes back to the kitchen and returns with a big glass of red wine, which he puts down on the coffee table before leaning in and giving me another kiss on the head. "I'll grab some towels and meet you in there once I've finished the girls' story."

I shovel the food into my mouth, appreciating the rich flavors bursting across my tongue, but I'm really ready to relax. Before long, I've finished, so I pick up both my glass and bowl and walk to the kitchen. Placing the bowl in the dishwasher, I continue out to the hot tub on the back patio with my glass of wine in hand. I set the glass on a nearby table and fold back the lid on the hot tub, then I peel my clothes off my weary body. Cold now that I'm naked, I hurry to grab my glass and climb carefully into the spa. When I'm comfortable, I push the button, and it roars to life, jets pulsing against all my tired, aching muscles.

"Fuck, that feels good," I mumble to myself as I lean my head back against the headrest. The heat and pressure of the hot tub relaxes my whole body, and I allow my mind to wander, settling on nothing in particular, but then I remember something from earlier in the day and sit up.

I meandered into the guys' office during our lunch break, hoping for a little nooky before the afternoon session. They were talking quietly and clammed up as soon as I walked in, and when I asked what the problem was, they refused to answer. They both also refused to sex me up, saying it wasn't professional. I was kind of hurt by that. It was okay when we were a secret and sneaking around, but now that people knew, it wasn't okay?

Both had quickly found other things to do.

I think maybe it's bothering me more than I thought it was, because now a hundred scenarios are playing over in my mind, mainly the one that tells me they are over having a curvy girl for a mate and are ready to go back to skinny bitches, or that they are ashamed of me and trying to find a way to break the mating. Neither of them could meet my eyes all afternoon.

The sound of the door closing has me opening my eyes and sitting up. Louis strides over to the tub with a mischievous grin on his face and quickly strips naked. Well, at least one of my mates wants me, I think as I study his gorgeous, naked body. He's not as bulky as Carter or Nolan. Louis is all long lean muscles, like a swimmer, and his cock juts out proudly, bobbing like it's waving hello. My mouth waters. I can't wait to have that inside me.

He climbs into the tub, his eyes heavy with heat, and slides over to me. Grabbing the glass of wine out of my hand, he takes a sip before putting it up on the edge, and then he pulls me toward him and lowers his lips to mine. They are soft and plush, and when his tongue seeks entrance, I give it to him gladly. He tastes like wine and sin, and I can't get enough as I wrap my arms around his shoulders and straddle him, grinding myself against his thick cock, both of us moaning with the sensations. I promised him a blow job, though, so instead of seeking my own pleasure, I climb off his lap and pat the side of the tub, gesturing for him to climb up. He just shakes his head and drags me back onto his lap.

"No, *mon sucre d'orge*, it is cold out, and I'd much rather bring you pleasure at the same time." He strokes my hair and kisses me again. "You've worked so hard this week, and I am so very proud of you. Let me ease some of your tension."

He rubs my shoulders, and I groan from how good it feels, then his hand slides down my chest, massaging the muscles and relieving some of the tension built up in there, before moving to my breasts. He cups them and runs his thumbs across my nipples, and my groan of relief turns into one of desire.

"Ride me, *mon amour*. Let me look into your eyes as we bring each other exquisite pleasure." Louis knows how much his French accent turns me on, and he really lays it on thick during sexy times, but who am I to argue with him? Rising up on my knees, I grab his thick length and notch it at my opening. Slowly, I work myself down over it, both of us breathing hard as I do, but finally, I'm seated all the way.

"Fuck, you feel good." I groan as I clench my inner muscles around him, my core throbbing with delight.

His eyes widen with the movement, and his hands go to my hips. With his help, I slowly work myself up and down on his fat cock, rolling my body so my clit brushes against his pelvis with every stroke, our eyes never leaving each other.

"Yeah, baby, just like that," Louis mutters. "Your pussy is squeezing my cock like a vise."

I love his dirty talk in that accent. A string of French words leaves his mouth, but I'm too lost in my pleasure to care about what he's saying. He could be sharing the grocery list for all I know, but it revs me higher and higher. I feel my orgasm building, that deep feeling inside my core that rises like a leviathan from the deep. My toes start to curl, and my breathing increases, the sounds of the spa drowning out the gasps and groans leaving our mouths.

Leaning in, I press my breasts against his smooth chest and fuse my mouth to his. The rolling pleasure arrives like a freight train, slamming into my body, and my pussy grips his cock tightly as my movements become frantic as I try to fuck him through my orgasm. Thankfully, he takes over and thrusts into me hard, his body taut with tension before he, too, finds his release. He shouts as it explodes from his body, shooting deep into my hot wet cunt. I slow my movements as we both ride out the wave of pleasure, our foreheads pressed together as our ragged breaths mix.

"Wow, I needed that. Thank you." I press another gentle kiss to my mate's mouth, reveling in the feel of his soft lips as his hands roam my back. My body is languid and relaxed, and I collapse against him, breathing in his scent that stands out above the odor of chlorine.

Louis's body stiffens slightly before he relaxes again, and I turn to see what startled him. Nolan stands in the shadows with his cock in hand, white strings of cum dripping off it. As annoyed as I am with him, I wish I'd been able to lick him while Louis fucked me, but I am gluttonous.

Nolan won't meet my eyes, though, and he quickly disappears back inside without a word. I slump against Louis with defeat, and he pushes me back until he's looking me in the eyes, his hand holding my chin.

"What is going on, Glory?" he demands, sounding confused. "Why was Nolan all shifty? Are you two in a fight?"

I shrug my shoulders in defeat. "Fuck knows, Louis. He and Carter have been avoiding me all day. They wouldn't even have a quickie with me in the office at lunch today."

His mouth drops open in surprise as he looks back to where Nolan disappeared.

"Carter hasn't been home in weeks. He keeps staying at his apartment above the club." I close my eyes as I ask my next question, not wanting to see his face when he answers. "What if they don't want me anymore? What if I'm just not enough for them?"

He shakes my shoulders. "Look at me, Glory," he demands gruffly, and I open my eyes to see him. He's the most serious I've ever seen. "That is far from the truth, they adore you. You're the best thing to ever happen to the three of us, and if I have to kick their asses to make them see that, then I will."

I shake my head as a tear rolls down my face,

and my heart aches. "No, Louis, I wouldn't want to force them to do anything they don't want to. Even if I have to go to Lucifer himself and ask him to break the mating, I will do that for them. A girl wants to be wanted and needed, not feel like a burden."

He growls again before standing up and climbing out of the tub, wrapping a towel around his waist. Louis holds out a hand and helps me out, draping a towel around me and picking me up bridal style.

"I don't think this is the case, but if so, then so be it. I will get to have you all to myself, and I can't get enough of you." He nuzzles the side of my neck as he carries me back inside and up to our bedroom, which is empty of Nolan.

We shower quickly to wash off the hot tub residue, and he dresses me in one of his shirts before he climbs into bed behind me, wrapping his arms around me and pulling my back into his chest. As my eyes drift closed, my exhaustion completely taking over, I hear him whisper, "Yes, having you as my mate is the best thing that has ever happened to me, and I will give you up for no one."

Chapter Ten

The next morning, I'm woken by two little giggling girls wriggling under my covers. Groaning, I pull the covers up over my head, and they giggle even harder. Thank goodness Louis thought to put a T-shirt on me before we went to bed. Normally, I'm up before everyone else, but I must have been even more exhausted than I thought.

"Mom, you said we were going to do stuff today," Aria scolds me as she tries to pull the covers out of my hands.

Zoe just snuggles into my back and wraps her little arms around my waist.

"Mom!" Aria demands sharply. I let go of the covers, and she tumbles backward.

Zoe giggles even harder as Aria frowns at the two of us. Rubbing a hand across my tired eyes, I finally look at the daughter of my heart, even if she's not from my body. She's dressed and ready to go with her hair braided, standing with her arms crossed and looking at me with an exasperated look that is way too old for a five-year-old.

Before she can scold me again, I reach up and

grab her, pulling her down into the bed with Zoe and me. I wrap my arms around her and pepper her little face with kisses.

"Why are you up so early? Most mornings I have to practically poke you with a stick to get you out of bed."

She's giggling now, but she places her hands on my cheeks and holds my face still. "It's ten o'clock, Mom. Uncle Louis said to let you sleep, and he made us breakfast and did our hair for us, but I'm tired of waiting. I want to go."

Oh wow, ten? It is late. "Okay, I'm sorry, I'll get up and get ready right away." Something occurs to me. "Why did Uncle Louis do your hair? Why didn't Daddy?"

Zoe jumps up and starts bouncing on the bed. "Daddy had to go to work this morning." She's smiling, not realizing the dread her words caused me.

Nolan never works on the weekend because he has the girls. He tries to make sure that he can spend all of that time with them. I guess he really is avoiding me. Well, that's fucked up. If those assholes want out of this mating, then I need to confront them. If that's the case, then they can tell me to my fucking face. We will need to apply to Lucifer to dissolve it, though that's going to hurt like hell, I realize, as I look at the two precious girls in front of me. I'm going to lose them. I'll go from

Mom to Aunty Glory if Louis stays true to his word. Fuck.

Swallowing the lump in my throat, I force a smile to my face. "Okay, go watch the *Puppy Patrol* or whatever it is and give me a chance to get ready, and then we will go."

"*Paw Patrol*, Mommy," Zoe corrects me, sounding exasperated and rolling her little eyes, but both girls bounce off the bed and run off to do as I asked.

Groaning, I slide out of bed and push my hair back from my face before wobbling into the bathroom to get ready. After peeing, I lean against the vanity and look at myself in the mirror. There are bags and dark circles under my eyes, and my normally lush hair looks dull and greasy. Peeling Louis's shirt off my body, I turn left and right, surveying my usual sumptuous curves. Over the last few weeks, I've lost weight, and I'm not happy with it. I'm obviously not eating as much food as I normally do, and it shows. Maybe that's why Nolan and Carter have lost interest.

I take a quick shower, washing my hair, before jumping out and drying myself off. Opting for comfy clothes of jeans, a T-shirt, and a pair of Converse, I towel dry my hair and braid it before heading downstairs for coffee.

When I get down there, Louis hands me a travel mug and my purse and shoos me out the door, giving me a kiss on the cheek. "I will see you at

Tasty Treats after you have finished the torture," he exclaims, and the girls giggle, following me out. I guess I don't have time for breakfast and can make up for it later at the buffet.

After strapping the girls into their seats, which are now in my car, I climb in and head for the nearest equestrian supplies store. The girls chat excitedly in the back about getting new things and the pony that my mom bought them. The pony's name is Saintly, and she lives up to her name, all sweetness and infinite patience, or so my dad Nic tells me. My mom has been picking them up from school and daycare since I have been doing my course, and she is loving having the girls around. All of them are, actually, even my brothers who still live at home, and the girls love their new family too. That sick feeling in my stomach comes back with a vengeance as I think about having to tell them it's all over because Carter and Nolan decided to break our mating. Fuck, there are going to be some very upset people on both sides if that's the case.

"Can I get a pink helmet, Mom?" Zoe asks from behind me. "Pink is my very favorite color."

Shaking off my gloom, I smile at her in the rearview mirror. "Of course you can, and pink is one of my very favorite colors too."

The trip to the equestrian store is fun, and I get the girls kitted out with helmets, pants, and boots, and when both of them look longingly at a glittery pink grooming set, I just have to buy them that as well.

As we get into the car to move on to Build-a-Bear, they bounce with excitement, but I decide to have the same conversation with them that my mom had with me when I got a pony.

"Now, it's wonderful that you guys have all this pretty new gear, but there's a lot of responsibility in owning an animal."

The girls fall silent and take on very serious expressions as they listen.

"It's not all about riding. They need to be fed and groomed, and their poop needs to be picked up too. These things will be your responsibility when you're at Grandma's place. Yes, Uncles Callen, Kade, Seth, or Silas would probably do it for you, but that's your pony, and you need to do the not so fun things too."

They both nod their heads. Aria seems keen to do everything, but Zoe not so much. "Poop too?" she questions quietly, and I grin in return.

"Yes, Zoe, poop too."

She shudders, and Aria starts to giggle.

"Zoe gags at the poop, Mom, but I don't care. It doesn't smell as bad as Max's poop."

Mom told me how well Aria was taking to all the jobs involved with the pony. Maybe Zoe is a little young, but she can still help out a bit.

"As long as you both try your hardest, I will be happy," I assure them.

Build-a-Bear is located in a mall close by, so it doesn't take us long to get there. With both girls holding my hands, and my purse slung over one shoulder, we walk through the mall to get to Build-a-Bear. Zoe tugs on my hand if I slow down to look at things in some of the store windows. Eventually, I give up and decide to come back at another time without them.

"Look, there it is!" Zoe shouts and drops my hand, running toward the blue and yellow storefront. Aria soon joins her, so I hurry after them but stop dead in my tracks as soon as I hit the store.

"Oh my god, I have entered hell."

The salesgirl straightening a nearby shelf snorts. "Yes, yes you have," she mutters quietly under her breath, but I pick it up with my supernatural hearing.

The store is full of running, screaming children and harassed-looking parents. I'd say it's a fifty-fifty split on happy children and ones who aren't getting what they want.

Lord, save me now. Please let Zoe and Aria be from the first category.

I watch as a child around the same age as Zoe throws themselves on the ground and starts wailing about not getting a heart. Holy shit. I scrub a hand across my eyes in disbelief and exchange a look of sympathy with the mother who appears to be on the brink of tears.

Stay strong, sister, you can do it.

The child brings out the big guns and starts pounding her fists on the ground. You know what? I'm just going to give Zoe and Aria whatever they want. If they want a heart, then we will have five. If they want an outfit, sure, knock yourselves out.

Hurrying through the crowd, I search for my girls. I find them both at the tubs of skins. Does anyone else think that a bunch of stuffed animal skins is just creepy as fuck? Like, how does anyone come up with the concept to start with? No, you know what? I don't even want to think about it.

Pasting a smile on my face, I listen to the girls discussing what they want. They are a little hard to hear over the noise, even with my enhanced hearing, but I listen to them arguing about outfits, wishes, and sounds. God, I think I'm out of my league here. No wonder Louis looked horrified when I told him where we were going. I can't believe he didn't say anything.

Looking around, I try to find someone to help us, but they are all busy, so I take a deep breath, plaster on a smile, and step between the arguing girls. "Okay, who's ready to build a bear?" I cheer, trying to distract the squabbling girls. They both jump up and down in response to my question. "So I guess we need to pick our skins," I say, looking at the row of tubs.

Aria picks up a white skin and holds it up for me. "I would like Olaf please." She sounds hesitant, making it sound like a question, and a little crease forms in her brow as she avoids meeting my gaze.

"If that's what you want, sweetie, then of course you can have it. You can have whatever you want." A small smile crosses her lips, and the wary look disappears as she hugs the skin to her chest.

"Oh, I want this one." Zoe holds up a multicolored pile of fur before flinging it away. "Oh no, I want this one." She runs to another box and pulls something else out before she gets distracted once again and runs to another box. "No, this one. This is definitely it," she tells me and holds up a pink skin with a shock of multicolored hair. "It's Poppy from *Trolls*, Mom," she shouts when I don't say anything.

"Oh, okay then, that's great." I'm glad she explained it to me, because I had no idea.

"What about you, Mom?" She jumps up and down on the spot, unable to stay still in her excitement.

"Me? You want me to build one too?"

They both nod with enthusiasm, so I wander along the display area, looking at all the ones they made for examples, when an idea comes to me. Picking up a light brown bear skin, I tuck it under my arm and look around the store.

All the sales assistants look busy, and I'm not sure what to do next, but I shouldn't have worried.

"To the stuffing machine!" Zoe shouts enthusiastically, but Aria shakes her head.

"No, we need to choose sounds." She drags us

over to a section of the store that has recordings that can go into the bears. Zoe chooses the one that sounds like Poppy from *Trolls*, and Aria chooses the one for Olaf. I decide not to put a voice in mine. From there, we line up behind a few families who are all waiting for the stuffing machine.

"Alright, gather around everyone," the Build-a-Bear person at the machine shouts. "We are going to stuff all your friends, and then we are going to do the heart ceremony all together. Make a line, and we will stuff the friends as quickly as possible. You can also grab a heart out of the heart box just there." She points to a box filled with red plastic hearts. All the kids run over and grab one, leaving their parents in line. The employee sits down on the machine, and the first bear is handed over. There are five children in front of Aria and Zoe, but the girl is efficient, and within ten minutes, everyone's bears are stuffed, including mine.

She switches off the machines and asks for all bears to be passed to a parent to care for during the heart ceremony.

"But what about you, Mom?" Aria asks, wearing a little frown on her face once more. "Who's going to hold our bears if you have to do the heart ceremony too?"

The employee hears her and comes over to us. "How about you just put them here on this table." She gestures behind the stuffing machine. "That way they will be safe while we do the ceremony."

Aria looks relieved, and the girls carry their friends and my bear over there before quickly returning to me. I mouth, "Thank you," to the employee, and she smiles at me with tired eyes before she starts the ceremony.

It's cute, and there are a whole heap of things that we need to do to our hearts so that our bears have all the traits that they need before we pop them into the back of the bear and pull up the zipper.

"Alright, now you need to head over to the fluffing stations and groom your bears, but because there are so many of you, why don't you three" — she points to me and the girls— "choose outfits first, and then you can swap before you dress them."

"Sounds good to me." I smile at the girl, and she smiles back with a relieved look on her face.

We do as she suggested, and Zoe picks out an outfit for Poppy, but Aria can't find anything that will fit Olaf, so she buys him a bed instead. Both girls are happy with their purchases and wait patiently to use the grooming station while I wander to find my bear some clothes.

"Can I help you with anything?" The relieved-looking salesgirl finally seems like she can breathe.

"Do you make custom outfits? Like, can I have a custom shirt made for my bear?"

She shakes her head. "No, unfortunately we don't do that at this stage, but..." She looks around and moves closer. "Between you and me, there are some people on Etsy who do that type of thing if you really want one."

I thank her, and we finish up our bears. I pay for them all before we head out. I'm starving and absolutely ready for Tasty Treats. The girls had some fries between the equestrian shop and Build-a-Bear, but they are ready to eat as well.

"Thank you so much, Mom. That was so much fun." Aria skips as we walk through the mall to the car.

I don't even want to stop and window shop after that experience. I think it will be a while before I come back, but then an idea hits me.

"It was fun, wasn't it? And you know who else would love that place? Grandma, and Uncles Callen, Kade, Seth, and Silas. You should ask each and every one of them to bring you."

The girls cheer, and I smile to myself. My work here is done. I'm just paying the love forward.

Tasty Treats is busy, but the staff loves Zoe and Aria, and each and every one of them come to our table and say hello to the girls. Louis is sitting with us when the other head chef comes out wheeling a cart. Like Louis, Gaspar is French too, but he is in his fifties, and with his round belly, white hair, and neatly trimmed white goatee, he could be Santa's sexy French brother.

"Ah, look who it is, my *préférée bèbès*. When Louis said that his pretty girls were coming in, I had an epiphany. Look what Uncle Gaspar has made for you today." His accent is a lot thicker than Louis's, and the girls giggle with delight.

The cart is covered with desserts that are obviously unicorn themed. There are unicorn cake pops, layered individual trifles with unicorn-colored custards, and unicorn macarons and biscuits, but in the middle is a giant fishbowl full of ice cream and sprinkles with a unicorn horn plonked into the middle of the lot.

"Ta-da, unicorn sundae for my best girls." He

picks it up and places it in the middle of the table and then hands us four spoons.

The girls squeal with delight. "Thank you, Uncle Gaspar," the girls say in unison before digging into the mountainous dessert.

True to his word, Louis had an Irish coffee waiting for me when we arrived. To be honest, I think it was more Irish than coffee, but I wasn't complaining after that experience. I smack him on the arm now that the girls are occupied.

"You could have warned me," I scold him as I take a big sip of my drink and shudder as the whiskey warms me all the way down.

He snorts. "And deprive you of that quintessential parenting experience? No thank you." He turns in the booth so he can look me in the eye. "Are you still going to the club with the girls tonight?" His brow is creased in concern, and I snuggle into him before answering.

"Yes." A big sigh escapes me. "I'm sick of tiptoeing around this. Have they said anything to you?"

He grunts and shakes his head. "No, it seems those assholes are avoiding me as well. After you fell asleep last night, I went looking for Nolan, but he must have left again. I looked at the security footage of the club on the computer, and it shows him entering our apartment there not long after we saw him, so he must have left straight after."

I shudder as I think about what might happen

tonight, and Louis grabs me and pulls me against him. "No matter what happens with them, I'm all in. We will find a place to live, just the two of us, and be perfectly happy without them," he tells me fiercely.

"But what about you guys? You are mates too. This is destroying all of us." I try to keep my tears in so I don't upset the girls, but he can hear it in my voice.

"Pfft, they will be missing out. How dare they do this to us? Secrets tear families apart, and if they have problems, they should talk to us, but do not worry, my sugar plum. I will be a very happy man even if it is just the two of us."

A few hours later, after a much needed nap once we arrived home, I am ready to go out with my new friends. I'm meeting both Kerry and Bella at the Garden of Eden, yet neither of them knows about the other. I'm parent trapping them—sort of. I can't wait to see their faces when they see one another.

The Uber I ordered drops me off in front of Carter's club, and as I step out of the car, I smooth down the dress I'm wearing. It's a cute, black, skater style dress with spaghetti straps and a plunging neckline. My boobs look amazing in it, and my legs look fucking fantastic with the four-inch heels I'm wearing. I figure I have to show the guys what they will be giving up if that happens to be the case. All they have seen me in recently are cargos, jeans, and Wrathful Bail Bonds shirts. Tonight they are going to swallow their tongues, if Louis's reaction was anything to go buy.

"Glory," he growled into my ear as he leaned down to kiss me goodbye. "Give me one reason why I shouldn't take you back upstairs, bend you over our bed, and slam my cock into that tight pussy of yours." His lips brushed against my cheek, and when he pulled away, I could see he was literally seconds from doing what he said. I patted him on his chest, feeling his pecs through his tight shirt.

"Because you want answers as much as I do. I can see that they are hurting you as much as they are hurting me. It's time, Louis, so we can go on with our lives." The heat in his eyes changed to sadness, and he nodded.

"Oui, you are right."

"Glory!" Hearing my name jolts me out of my memories, and a smile crosses my lips as I notice Kerry and Bella standing just in front of the club together.

I clap my hands and hurry over. "Ah, I see you both found my surprise."

They have their arms linked and look thrilled to see each other.

"You sneaky bitch," Bella says, slapping my arm. "I haven't seen Kerry in years. I can't believe she's topside doing this course. Thank you, Glory, for this. My wedding made me realize that all the friends I have, apart from Lizzie, are not really friends. Those other bitches were just bad luck, and, well, I'm not easy to get along with because of my wrath side. Human women tend to pick up the vibes, even if they don't know exactly what it is about me that they are wary of. This is a real blessing." Bella drops Kerry's arm and envelops me in a hug before pulling away.

"Hey!" Kerry smiles at me. "You still look exhausted. Are those assholes still being difficult?"

"Yeah." I smile ruefully.

Kerry noticed them becoming more and more distant all week.

"That, and I took the girls to Build-a-Bear today. Trust me on this, don't ever do it."

Bella snorts with laughter. "Oh, I've been there, and I won't be doing that again anytime soon."

"Don't worry, I told the girls that my family will gladly take them. I think we're probably good for at least a year."

Both women laugh, and we head toward the big, beefy bouncer manning the door of the club. Behind a rope is a long line of people waiting to get in, but Bella just ignores them.

"Hi, Mac, have you been busy tonight?" Bella asks, and the beefy dude nods his head.

"Sure have been. Does your husband know you're here tonight?" he teases, talking to Bella like they are old friends.

"Felix is meeting me here later." She winks, and

he chuckles. "This is Glory." She gestures to me, and the big guy's eyes almost bug out of his head, but he smiles and puts out a hand.

"Nice to meet you, Glory. I'm Mac, head of security. Carter's talked about you a lot, but he didn't say you were coming in tonight."

I take his big mitt in mine and shake it, smiling at him. "It's a secret. I was hoping to surprise him."

He runs a hand over his bald head and chuckles. "Oh, I think you're going to definitely do that. I won't even tell him."

The girls and I exchange a glance. What does that mean?

"Thanks, I appreciate it," I tell him as he unclips the rope and lets us through.

If he's implying I'll be interrupting something, well, I just so happened to put my Taser in my purse again. They better hope they are alone when I find them, or they will feel the wrath of Sparky before I kick them to the curb.

"What was that about?" Bella asks as we step up to the bar, and my gaze wanders around the club, not really absorbing anything in my worried state.

"Carter and Nolan have been avoiding Glory for a week or two, and she says they haven't had sex in weeks. Carter isn't even coming home, instead staying here overnight, and Nolan comes but he's barely been in their bed. It's just been her and Louis."

"What the fuck?" Bella's eyes blaze as her wrath

demon comes out to play. "Let's get you a drink, and then we'll find your mates and kick their asses," she growls as she waves a hand at the bartender.

When he wanders over with a smile, I do a double take. Silas takes a cloth and rubs a wet mark off the bar in front of us before asking, "What can I get you beautiful ladies?"

"How are you here?" I blurt, waving my hand at my brother.

"You know this guy?" Bella asks, eyeing my brother with appreciation. Although they are young, they don't look it, and even I can acknowledge that my brothers are hot.

"Bella, Kerry, meet my brother Silas." I wave between them all, and the girls stare at me before waving at him. "Kerry is in my class, and Bella is Nolan's sister.

"Awesome, more family." He yawns, blushing as he puts his hand over his mouth. "Sorry, it's taking a while to get used to this, but the lust from downstairs helps," he tells me, and the girls look at me for an explanation.

"Silas and his twin brother, Seth, are sloth demons with a side of lust like me." I turn back to my brother. "But what are you doing here? When did you start working here and where is Seth?"

He smiles broadly. "Carter called us a few days after we met and offered us jobs. Callen and Kade are here too. Callen is working in one of the bars downstairs, and Kade is bouncing—his spot is over on the dance floor. Both of them will be doing the next course Nolan and Carter run, so this is just for now."

My eyes widen as he tells me everything, and my heart sinks even more as I realize that Carter and Nolan really haven't been telling me a thing.

"Oh." My voice comes out smaller than I planned, and he frowns at me.

"Are you okay, Glory?" he asks, and I wave my hand at him.

"I'm fine." I don't want to tell him what is going on and worry him, not to mention he would get straight on the phone to Mom and blab, and then all hell would break loose. "Where's Seth? You told me where the others are, but you didn't mention him."

He looks a little uncomfortable and shifts on his feet. "Um, well, that's because he's downstairs."

"Okay, so what?"

Silas looks to Bella for help, and she snorts. "Well, that's the sex dungeon."

My eyes just about bug out of my head. "So both Callen and Seth are working the bar downstairs?" I ask my brother, and he squirms. "What aren't you telling me, Silas?" I growl.

"Carter is training Seth to be a dungeon master." The words come out in a rush.

"So? Aren't they just the supervisors of the club who make sure nothing goes wrong?"

"Yeah, but Carter insists that if Seth is going to

police the floor, then he needs to get a firsthand feel at what he's policing."

"Are you telling me that Seth is downstairs playing in the dungeon?"

He nods quickly before running away to serve someone else.

"Damn it, we didn't even get a drink," Bella complains and goes down to the end of the bar, leaving me gaping and speechless.

Kerry is studying me. I think she's trying to work out if I'm going to pass out or explode. I breathe in deep in an attempt to control my anger.

"Look, they are big boys. Carter wouldn't be making them do anything they don't want to do. This place is big on consent, everyone's consent," Bella says from the other side of the bar as she expertly mixes us some kind of concoction.

"Make mine a double," I growl, and she laughs.

"Don't worry, Glory, I've got you. Anyway, Seth will be getting a feel for the operations downstairs and what he's comfortable with. If he's uncomfortable, he won't be suitable, and that will be that. Carter can be an asshole, but he wouldn't put your brothers at risk, I promise," she assures me, and I know what she's saying is true, but I can't help but worry, which I guess is hypocritical after I let Carter and Nolan do those things to me weeks ago.

Fuck, I can't believe it has been a month already.

"I'm not upset about the fact that my little

brother is probably downstairs railing on someone, more the fact that Carter didn't tell me."

"Here, drink this. You'll feel better." She slides a drink in front of me that's bright blue in color but has a sparkle like glitter has been sprinkled through it.

"What is it?" I ask, taking a sip. The drink hits my taste buds, and they sing with joy. "Whoa, this is delicious."

"Wow, where did you get devil dust from?" Kerry asks after taking a sip of her drink.

"Devil dust?" I ask, looking between them, and Bella gestures for Kerry to tell the story.

"It's a drug made in Hell. It's the crushed form of a fungus that grows in caves underneath Lucifer's palace. The right amount is used to keep violent prisoners docile, but when added to human alcohol, it has somewhat of a different effect," she explains as my body starts to tingle like I'm bathing in sparkling water. It tickles, and a giggle bubbles out of my mouth.

"It relaxes you and leaves you feeling mellow, usually chilling your demon side out. The only ones who shouldn't take it are lust demons, but if they do, then they are in for some fun."

The tickle turns into a throb, and I feel something pulse deep within my core. A moan escapes my mouth as Bella raises an eyebrow.

"I thought you were a gluttony demon, Glory?" she asks, giggling.

"Yeah, but Mom's a lust demon, and I got a good dose of that too somehow. In fact, all of us are more like half-and-half, which shouldn't be possible." I start to pant, and she frowns.

"Who is your mom, Glory?" Kerry asks, her brow wrinkled with worry.

I giggle and use my finger to smooth out the lines, but I almost poke her in the eye instead. "Petra Luxure."

Kerry's eyes widen. "Holy shit."

Bella's wearing a confused look, which I'm sure is mirrored on my face.

"What's wrong? You know my mom?" I ask her as I try not to touch myself.

Kerry puts her drink down and drags me across the club with Bella in tow. "What's wrong with her, Kerry?"

"Petra Luxure is Lucifer's sister. They had a falling out years ago, and she hasn't been below in a long time. That's the reason you are strong in both traits. Petra's that powerful. If we don't get you to your mates before that completely kicks in, then we are in for a world of trouble."

Bella pushes past us and hurries to the elevator, jabbing at the button as I giggle, sway, and moan. Fuck, I'm all over the place. My body feels light as a feather, and Kerry's hand on my arm causes goose-bumps to erupt. Unlike my sister, I've never been interested in girls, but right at this moment, both Bella and Kerry are looking mighty fine.

"I'll take her to a room while you find Carter or Nolan and let them know what's going on," Bella instructs Kerry, who nods, but I shake my head.

"No, not those assholes. Call my freaky French fuckboy," I demand, my voice echoing through the elevator as it descends.

As the doors open, the smell of sex and debauchery hits me, and I groan, clenching my thighs together in the hopes it will relieve some of the pressure between them.

Kerry leaves us as Bella drags me through a scantily clad crowd. Just like upstairs, there's a dance floor with writhing bodies, but unlike upstairs, there are sexual acts taking place on the dance floor. Out of the corner of my eye, I watch a bent over woman sucking a man's cock as she's thrust into from behind by another.

That's all I get to see before Bella leads me into a door lined corridor. "These are all private rooms. The light above it tells us if it's occupied or not. Red means occupied, and green means empty," she tells me as she leads me to one at the end without a light above it. "This is Carter's private room. The guys have an apartment above the club, but we don't have time to get you up there. You'll start pumping out those lust hormones any minute now, and it will be a free-for-all." She opens the door and pushes me through. "Wait here."

The door closes behind me, and as I look around the room, I recognize the same setup that they have in the secret room at home. Conflicting feelings rush through me. On one hand, I'm horny as fuck, and on the other, I'm furious with jealousy. How many people have been through this room before me?

Rolling my eyes at myself, I toe off my shoes and take another sip of the drink the girls failed to take away from me. Fuck it, I'm going all in. I have everything I need to get myself off, so maybe I should just lock the door, grab one of those dildos, and take care of my own needs.

Walking around the room, I run my finger over the various instruments hanging on the wall before climbing up on the large bed covered in blood-red pillows. The whole room is set up for seduction. There are shackles on all four corners of the bed, as well as a huge mirror across from it, and one on top of the ceiling. I fluff my hair a little in the reflection before blowing myself a kiss and giggling. My hands brush against my nipples, and I moan from the sensation. Holy shit, I don't think I've ever been this turned on in my life. Trying to distract myself from the feeling, I grab the remote control that's on the bedside table. Maybe watching some TV will distract me. There are only two buttons on the remote, which is weird, but I press one anyway and scream as the mirror in front of me becomes opaque, showing me the room on the other side.

Holy shit, I turn my head sideways as I try to figure out the view in front of me. There are limbs and naked body parts everywhere. It's most definitely an orgy and not helping the lust that's flowing through my body at all. I slip one of my hands into my panties and slowly circle the throbbing nub of my clit, trying to relieve some of the pressure. I quickly press the button again, and the mirror goes back to the way it was. Maybe I'd make use of it another day, but not today. Nope, Kerry went to get Nolan and Carter, and I am going to have a face-to-face conversation about what the fuck is going on. No sex, just talking.

But my fingers feel so good on my clit. I moan and squirm and eye the row of dildos on the shelf over on the wall. It would serve them right if they found me taking care of myself. I mean, I don't think they'd want my body to ache like it does, even if they don't want to be with me. I rub my clit a little harder and scissor my legs open and closed, trying to make the empty feeling go away.

My mind is a chaotic mess, and I sob, wishing that my mates were here to take care of the incessant need thrumming through my body. My skin itches where my dress touches it, so I peel it over my head and throw it away, leaving me in only my panties. My breath is fast, but my orgasm seems to be stalled. Why can't I come? I've never had this problem before. The tears leaking down my cheek stimulate my oversensitive skin even more, and I cry out in frustration just as the door opens and Carter and Nolan enter, both looking concerned.

They rush over to the bed and climb on. "Oh, baby, that's never going to work," Carter croons, reaching out for me. "Devil dust in a lust demon needs to be relieved by someone else's hands."

I screech and hold up the hand that's not in my panties. "No, don't touch me."

They sit back on their heels and look at each other in shock.

"What's wrong, Glory?" Nolan asks carefully.

"You fuckers have avoided me for weeks." I pant through the need then grit my teeth. I'll get this out, and if I need to, I'll wait until Louis can get here. "You haven't touched me, and you went out of your way not to be near me, especially you." I point a finger at Carter. "Do you not want to be my mates anymore? Should we go to Hell to ask Lucifer to end it?"

Both guys' eyes widen in surprise. "What the fuck, Glory?" Carter growls at the same time Nolan shouts, "Fuck no!"

"Why would you think we want out of the

mating?" Nolan asks, reaching out for my leg, but I slap his hand away as I still rub furiously at my clit.

"Where have you been? Why don't you love me anymore?" I cry, the desperation becoming too much, and I break into heaving sobs, still working my hand.

The guys ignore my attempts to push them away and surround me. "Let us take care of this for you, Glory, and then we will explain everything. I promise that there's no one else, and we don't want out of this mating," Carter whispers in my ear as he strokes my hair, and Nolan snuggles me from behind.

I nod, unable to get the words out, and Carter rolls me onto my back and moves down the bed, pulling my panties off. He pushes my hand away and buries his face in my pussy. One lick is all it takes for me to explode. I feel myself squirt, and Carter laps it all up, rumbling in approval. "Yeah, baby, that's it, give it to me. I love wearing you on my face." His voice vibrates against my pussy, sending more shockwaves up my spine.

Nolan kisses me before moving down to bite and suck my nipples, prolonging my orgasm. As my breathing eases, he stops and looks at me. "The only real way to relieve the devil dust is to fuck, Glory. Tell us what you want."

I think about what I saw during the orgy. "I want Carter to fuck me while you fuck him," I demand, my voice a little hoarse from screaming during my first orgasm.

Nolan grins and rolls off the bed, grabbing some lube off the shelf. "Anything for you, baby. It's not a hardship at all."

Carter pulls his mouth away from my pussy and turns me over before hauling my hips up so I'm on my hands and knees. Then, he turns us so we are facing the mirror. Carter rubs his hands over my back, his rough calluses causing me to whimper and moan as my need comes back with a vengeance.

"Oh, I thought it was gone," I cry out, and he places kisses along my spine.

"No, baby, only my cum will stop the need. Lust demons are taught early on to stay away from devil's dust or make sure they have a willing partner or three around, but I guess no one thought it would ever affect you like this."

I watch as Nolan moves behind Carter. I can't see what he is doing, but Carter grunts and closes his eyes in pleasure, so I'm assuming Nolan is prepping him.

Scrambling around, I take Carter's thick cock into my mouth, sucking hard, and he moans before pushing me away. "Turn around, Glory," he demands, narrowing his eyes as heat flares in his gaze.

I turn back around, my eyes on the mirror as I watch Carter line himself up and thrust forward. "Fuck!" I scream as his fat cock invades my tight channel. My eyes water a little at the pain, but it ebbs as my pussy flutters in joy.

"God, Glory, your cunt squeezes my cock so good," Carter says through gritted teeth as he leans over me, and I watch in the mirror as Nolan eases into Carter's ass. Both of us are panting now, and I'm squirming on Carter's cock, but he sits up and slaps my ass. "Be a good girl and be patient."

I watch as Nolan turns Carter's head, and they kiss as Nolan thrusts twice. Each time, I feel Carter's cock jump inside me, and I moan in pleasure. They pull apart, and Nolan pushes Carter down over me again.

Our eyes meet in the mirror, and he starts to thrust gently into Carter as he thrusts into me. We all moan at the sensations as Carter's hand comes around, and he rolls my clit between his fingers.

"Faster and harder," I beg Nolan in the mirror, and a wicked grin crosses his face.

"Anything for you." He grips Carter's hips hard and starts to rail him, which causes Carter's cock to do the same to me. My head hangs, and I lose eye contact as I moan at the pleasure. I struggle to hold myself up, but I want to watch as both my lovers go over the edge. It's like a chain reaction. My orgasm detonates, and my pussy clamps down hard on Carter's cock. I feel the ripples of my inner walls as they spasm around him. He shouts, and I feel his cum explode out of his tip and hit my walls as Nolan moans and stills, buried deep in Carter's ass.

"Fuck yes," I scream as my orgasm continues to roll over me. My arms give way, and I collapse onto the bed below, the sheets muffling my cries of joy.

"Fuck, Glory, your pussy has me trapped," Carter growls in delight.

A hand on my head has me looking up. Nolan is in front of me now, and he takes my mouth with his as Carter continues to be locked into my orgasm. His fingers pluck my nipples as his chest warms my back. All the sensations are too much, and I black out.

When I wake up, I'm tucked into the bed with the sheets pulled up around me, keeping my body warm. I'm fucking exhausted. I feel like I've been run over by a truck, and they stopped and put it into reverse to make sure they really got me. Every single part of my body aches, and even opening my eyes is a struggle. I can't stop the whimper that leaves my mouth as I roll onto my back. A deep chuckle has me trying to lift my head, but it hurts too much, so I stop.

"Can't move," I grumble, and the bed dips as Nolan sits down next to me in my line of sight.

He pushes my hair out of my face for me, his eyes filled with love and sympathy. "Devil dust is a bitch to recover from for lust demons. The high is extreme, but it really doesn't make the next day any easier. Every other kind of demon is fine and doesn't have any adverse effects. Carter went to get you something to drink to help replenish your energy and dull the ache."

I hear the door open as he says this, and Carter appears on the other side of the bed, holding a tray in his hands, which he puts down on the bedside table. "Hey, baby, if you sit up, you can drink this, and you'll feel better."

I try, but nothing happens. "Can't," I croak, and they both lean in and help me up.

Nolan holds me as Carter fluffs pillows to support me. Once they get me situated, Carter hands me a glass with another concoction I don't recognize. It's thick and sludgy and smells bad. I lift an eyebrow in question, and even that hurts.

"Don't ask what it is, just drink it and drink it quickly. It will counteract the aftermath of the devil dust… Well, it will make you feel a little better. You'll need to sleep the rest of it off. You'll be fine by tomorrow."

My gaze sweeps the room in search of some hint of the time. "But I'm supposed to be hanging out with Bella and Kerry."

Nolan strokes my hair again as Carter holds the glass up to my mouth. "Don't worry about them, they are fine. Bella feels incredibly guilty, but none of us knew how strong your lust side was. We probably should have guessed it from the fact that you have three mates," Nolan assures me as I drink the sludge.

I brace for the taste and almost gag as it hits my taste buds, but I manage to swallow it all down. Carter hands me a glass of water to wash it down. "Good girl," he praises as I finish it, and then he takes both glasses away.

The guys help me settle down and then join me on either side. I look between them, unsure where we stand at the moment. They must see my wariness because they exchange a glance, and Nolan sighs.

"Oh, baby, there's been a lot going on that you don't know about, and neither of us were quite sure how to tell you. I guess we found it easier to avoid you than admit what was wrong."

My heart skips a beat as a ton of random ideas run through my head, and I start to panic.

They must be able to see it, because they both reach for me. Nolan cups my cheek, and Carter picks up my hand and places a kiss on my palm.

"Shh, it has nothing to do with us and our mating. We're in this for life, no matter what," Carter assures me, and a huge sigh of relief escapes my mouth before I can stop it.

"So why have you been avoiding me?" I ask quietly.

"I'm afraid we've failed you." Nolan sounds distraught, so I look to Carter.

"We promised you that when Bridgette was caught, she would be locked up and never let out again, but we got word not long after you started the course that she, her lawyer, and the two bumbling idiots were all granted bail, pending a trial. Someone paid that bail, and they are now out. When we aren't at work, Nolan and I have been busy keeping an eye on them, tracking all their movements to make sure they don't come anywhere near you or the girls."

"But Louis didn't know this either," I argue, and they both shake their heads.

"Louis has a terrible poker face and major guilt about lying." Nolan chuckles. "You would have been the first person he admitted it to. Never tell Louis something you want kept secret."

I giggle at that, but I'm still pissed. "I'm not a child. I know you want to protect me, but all it did was drive a wedge between us and make Louis and me panic. No more secrets, we're in this together. How do you think you made Louis feel? You guys have been together a lot longer than all of us, and you chose not to trust him. I know he's feeling as hurt as I am about this. He said he would be done with you if you two were going to break the mating."

Panic crosses their faces, and Nolan runs a hand over his chin in worry. "Fuck, we really screwed up. We will talk to him. You're right, neither of you deserved to be treated that way."

"We were idiots. I promise this will never

happen again," Carter pleads, and I decide to let it go. Yeah, they hurt us both, but I think they realize it, and hopefully it won't happen again.

"Don't let it happen again. I won't be so forgiving next time," I warn them.

Again, they exchange a mysterious glance. Carter nods, and Nolan breathes out an aggravated sigh. "While we're in full disclosure mode, I have to tell you that the two brothers who actually took you have disappeared. They were supposed to appear in court this week and never showed up. We have been contracted to chase them down by the bond company that put up their bail."

I struggle to sit up, and the guys give me a hand. The pain is starting to ease, but my muscles still aren't fully cooperating. "I want in!" They start to argue, but I stop them. "No, stop it. That was what we were doing this week, helping with leg work on actual cases, and then going on ride-alongs. I want this case. Please, I deserve it."

I know they are going to agree before they even say it, so I make grabby movements with my hands and kissing noises with my mouth. They both chuckle and come down so I can kiss them both. It's a three-way kiss that is hot and tempting, but I'm still too sore to attempt anything else, so I drag them down beside me, close my eyes, and smile, content with my lot in life again.

"Sleep now, and tomorrow, you can show me more of this club," I murmur, and then I remember something, my eyes popping open. "And you can tell me what the fuck my brothers are all doing working here and why I'm only just finding out about it."

They both blanch. "Yes, Glory," they chorus, looking a little nervous, and I smile again.

That's the right answer.

We spend the next week tracking the Slater brothers' movements—the two idiots whom I managed to get the best of after they kidnapped the girls and me at gunpoint.

They have been surprisingly good at hiding, but we finally tracked them down, and now Carter and Nolan are leading two teams to apprehend them. There's Nolan and Carter as well as two other experienced agents, and then there's Kerry, myself, and, unfortunately, BJ and Jeff.

"I can't believe this is where they are hiding," Jeff scoffs as we all stand in front of the place. "Drag show" flashes in neon lights above us, announcing to the world what this place is.

"It's ingenious, really," Kerry muses. "Nobody is going to look twice at two men dressing up at a drag show. They are perfectly disguised in plain sight."

I shudder at the thought of what those two guys would look like in drag.

"So how are we going to recognize them?" BJ asks as we approach the entrance, and Carter pulls the bouncer aside to talk to him.

I laugh as I think about the two men. "I guarantee they are the two ugliest ones in there."

Carter returns and starts issuing instructions. "Okay, there's only one exit. I want Jeff, BJ, Sam, and Dean to head around back and wait in case they catch wind of us. Kerry and Glory, you're with us. Glory will be able to identify them because she's actually had contact with them. Remember, you guys are here to observe only. Don't engage unless it's absolutely necessary. We don't know if they are carrying weapons. We've found that if people are going to make such an effort to hide, then they are pretty damn desperate and will resort to any measures not to be apprehended. Keep your wits about you, and remember we don't want to make it too obvious. We don't want to spook them and have them bolt."

Nolan takes over. "We have another skip we got a location for after this, so once these two are apprehended, Sam and Dean will take BJ, Jeff, and Kerry and show them how the delivery process goes. Glory will come with Carter and me while we detain the other one. It's pretty straight forward and should be a simple apprehension."

Everyone agrees to the plan, and we get moving.

When we get inside, the club is set up in a dinner theater style with lots of tables and booths facing a main stage with the bar directly opposite. A hostess approaches us and offers to show us to a table, which we accept. When we get there, she leaves us with a menu and a smile, assuring us she will be back shortly.

The four of us pretend to look over the menu while also scoping out the situation. The club is packed with well-dressed patrons all waiting for the show to start. Wait staff buzzes between the tables, taking orders and delivering food and drinks. A couple of drag queens saunter through the crowd, engaging people in small talk and generally keeping the crowd entertained. It's noisy and loud, and I would love to come back someday when we're not looking for fugitives.

"Any sign of them?" Carter asks after putting his finger up to the earpiece he's wearing.

"Negative," I hear one of the other teams respond. I don't recognize the voice, so it must be either Sam or Dean. I don't know them well enough to pinpoint which.

"Roger that," Carter replies.

"Glory, I want you to go to the restroom and have a look around. See if you can identify a dressing room or something where all the performers are getting ready," Nolan instructs, and I nod just as a waitress steps up to our table.

"What can I get you all?" she asks with a polite smile on her face.

"Can you point me in the direction of the restroom?" I ask her, smiling brightly.

"Sure! See the restroom sign just to the side of

the stage?" She points, and I follow her hand. "Head through the door, and the ladies' room is the last on the left. Don't go right, because that's the dressing room for the entertainment."

I thank her and leave the others to place an order while I head in the right direction.

"Remember, Glory, if you see them, stay out of sight and let us know." Carter's voice echoes in my ear, and I wince slightly, almost stumbling into a tall, gorgeous drag queen.

She steadies me, grabbing hold of my denim-clad arm. "You okay, love?" she asks me, looking concerned, her long eyelashes fluttering madly, and I smile brightly at her.

"Yeah, sorry, I'm clumsy and tripped. God, you're gorgeous," I gush as I look her up and down, and a blinding smile crosses her face.

She has gorgeous red hair, Jessica Rabbit style, with a green, turtlenecked, sequin dress which flows like a waterfall over her lush breasts, hugging her curves before splitting just below the crotch, allowing a glimpse of her shapely legs. Her makeup is on point, with her gray eyes accentuated by long, beautiful lashes and smoky eye makeup. Her lips are pouty and plush, slicked with red lipstick.

"Aww, aren't you a sweetie? You're pretty hot stuff yourself," she exclaims huskily, and then I think of something.

"Hey, maybe you can help me. Has the show acquired any new performers recently?"

Her expression changes to disgust as she curls her lip. "Yes, and they are an embarrassment. I don't know where the boss found them, but they are some of the worst drag queens I have ever seen," she says, smoothing out her dress in agitation. Her long nails pluck an invisible piece of lint from the perfect fabric. "They are going to make us all look terrible. Nobody's going to want to come back and see us if they are in it," she whines.

"Can you point me in their direction? I'll make sure that never happens."

Her eyes light up, and she grabs my arm, dragging me toward the restroom doors. "Our dressing room is on the right. Both of them should be in there. They are taking forever to get dressed, and I'm not even sure they know what they are doing with their makeup."

When she pushes the door open, I see it leads into a long corridor. On the left are signs for the restrooms, but on the other side are two doors. One reads, "Stage Entrance," the other says, "Dressing Room."

"Thank you. If you go back out and pretend you know nothing, I'll get my crew to come remove the problem for you."

She pauses at this and frowns. "By get rid of the problem, you don't mean kill them, do you?"

A laugh escapes me, and I shake my head. "No, we're fugitive recovery agents, and they are wanted."

Her mouth purses in surprise. "Oh, I knew there was something fishy about them. Just inside the door is a privacy screen, so you can sneak up on them. Good luck, gorgeous." She disappears in a rustle of sequins, leaving me in the corridor on my own.

I press a finger to my ear, approaching the right door. "I found them. They are both in the dressing room and are on their own at the moment. We're not going to get a better time."

"Roger that. Stand down, Glory, we'll take it from here," Carter says, and I step back from the door, a pang of disappointment hitting me, but I need to listen to the bosses.

Before I can reply, however, the door flings open.

"I have to piss before I put on that fucking dress." Randy steps out of the room, his thick body almost naked apart from a pair of tights, which are pulled up over his beer belly, a padded bra, and a skull cap. His skin is pasty white under the thick rug of black hair covering his body. I huddle against the wall in the hope he won't actually meet my eyes, but it's too late. We make eye contact, and his just about bulge out of his head.

"You!" he shouts before turning and throwing himself through the door he just exited. "Chuck, the gig's up, we need to bail. We've been found!"

I stop for a moment, looking at the door to the

restaurant, but it doesn't open with the others, so I make a snap decision.

"We've been made. Fugitives are on the run. I'm going to pursue," I shout as I follow Randy, pulling Sparky from the holster hidden under my denim jacket.

"No, Glory, you don't know if they have guns," Nolan yells.

"Wait, we're trying to get through, but the show started, and there's a fucking conga line blocking us," Carter growls.

When I get into the change room, it's a drag queen's paradise, smelling of sweet perfume and powder with sequins and feathers draped every-where. The two men standing in the middle completely ruin the aesthetic.

"Where the fuck did you come from?" Chuck shouts, wearing a sequined dress stuck halfway around his hips.

"Stay the hell away from me, you she-devil." Randy holds up his fingers in the sign of the cross. Oh, they haven't even begun to see my demon yet.

"Freeze, motherfuckers, you're surrounded." I know, cliché as fuck, but I've been dying to say it.

"Like hell," Randy shouts, picking up a container and hurling it at me.

White powder billows across the room as the two idiots turn and bolt in the opposite direction. Waving my hand, I cough as I move through the cloud of scented powder, thinking that I've cornered them, only to discover there's another exit. That can't be right. That wasn't on the plans, but when I pull the door open, it leads to a set of stairs, and I can see Chuck still shuffling up them, the dress constricting his movements.

"Hurry, Chuck," Randy screams, looking back at me and dragging his brother.

I run up the stairs and burst out onto the stage where there's an ensemble act singing, "We Are Family." Falsies, both eyelashes and boobs, abound, as I try to follow Chuck and Randy through the forest of drag queens. I'm not short, but these women are all wearing skyscraper high heels, and they practically dwarf me.

"Glory, where are you?" Kerry shouts through my earpiece. "Carter and Nolan are fighting their way backstage."

"Fuck, I'm on the stage now. They are trying to make a run for it. I think they are going for the front door."

I trip suddenly and fall onto one of the drag queens, my face landing in their very ample cleavage and my body landing on top of theirs. As I look up into their gray eyes, I feel a stirring in the pelvic region under their sequined dress. It's the same one I had run into beforehand, but she doesn't look too upset at the situation.

"Well, hello again, honey," she purrs at me as I

struggle to get up and keep an eye on the two getting away from me. I'm not sure where to put my hands, and I keep slipping and falling back onto her. She doesn't do anything to help. In fact, I kind of get the feeling she really likes it.

"Can you please help me?" I shout in frustration. "They are getting away." I put my finger to my ear. "I'm down and have lost sight of them. Can anyone confirm a visual?"

"I've got them," Kerry shouts, "but they saw me, and they are headed back in your direction."

"Fuck." Rolling onto my back and off of the woman, I struggle to my feet, but she's quicker, even in her sky-high heels, and once up, she offers me her hand.

Grasping it, I start to pull myself up when time stops. A sharp sting in my hand has me pausing in surprise and looking down. My mate mark is glowing, and it now has another ring around it—green, an envy demon. When I look up, she appears just as shocked as I do, and she is staring at our hands in horror.

"Mate? You're my mate? I don't understand this. I can't have a mate," she sputters, still in character as she looks between the mark and me. "I haven't had a girlfriend in years!"

Ouch, that kind of hurts. Does that mean she doesn't want me?

A commotion behind her draws my attention,

and I peer around her to see what's going on. Chuck and Randy are coming at us—Chuck with a champagne bottle in his hand, and Randy with a broken champagne flute. Their expressions are feral with desperation, and a battle cry sounds out across the stage. The music shuts off abruptly, so the sound bounces around the now silent club. In what feels like slow motion, I push the delicious queen out of the way and aim Sparky, which I still have clutched in my left hand, at Chuck who is in front. Pulling the trigger, I watch as the prongs shoot out and lodge into his naked chest, sending fifty thousand volts into him. He goes down hard in front of Randy, who falls over his brother and lands on top of him, much like I did just minutes before.

"Stay down. Don't make me shoot you too," I scream at him, but he doesn't listen.

He scrambles to his feet, so without hesitation, I shoot my Taser again, and the second set of prongs hits him, sending electricity coursing through his body. He lands on top of his brother, and I watch as a pool of liquid stains his tights.

"Who are you?" I hear the breathy voice from behind me, and I turn to find my new mate staring at me, wide-eyed and a little wary.

"I'm Glory, fugitive recovery agent and just plain badass," I tell her as Kerry slides to stop next to the pile of twitching brothers. Carter and Nolan finally make their way up the back steps and stop, their mouths gaping open at the carnage around me.

"Well, hello." The drag queen recovers quickly and flutters her eyelashes at them.

I roll my eyes as they look between me and the brothers. Carter pulls out a pair of handcuffs, and my new mate twitters in excitement. He and Kerry proceed to roll the brothers onto their stomachs and cuff both of them as Nolan comes over to me.

"Are you okay?" He grabs my face between his hands. "We felt what happened. Who is it?" I wave my hand in the direction of my new mate, who waves flirtatiously at him, and his eyes widen in surprise. "Oh."

"Yeah, she didn't look too thrilled either." My emotions are all over the place. On one hand, I'm stoked that we got the brothers, and on the other, I'm confused about my new mate and what to do about her… him… them? Has the universe fucked up and given me a mate who has no interest in the female sex, or is this an act they put on when in drag? Fuck, just when I fixed my mate problems with the other two, the universe decides I haven't had enough.

"Come on, let's get these guys out front so the others can take them in. We have that other one we need to track down."

"What about me?" The voice is slightly timid, unlike her boisterous attitude from before.

Nolan pulls a card out of his pocket. "This is

where you can find us during the week. Think about what you want, and then give us a call when you decide. There's a way out of this if you really don't want it." Nolan's voice is neutral as he hands her the card before grabbing my arm and guiding me over to Kerry and Carter, who are trying to get the brothers up.

We scramble to give them a hand, and eventually, we have both of them on their feet. As we lead them away, I turn to look at my new mate, and she looks lost as her friends gather around her to make sure she's okay. The card is still in her hand, and her eyes look sad, but she doesn't stop me from leaving.

Shrugging, I turn back and pay attention to what we're doing. She will either come to me or she won't. I have had enough mate worries to last me a lifetime.

As I reach them and help Nolan lift Randy to his feet, his head tips to the side and he slurs at me, his eyes rolling around in their sockets.

"You're a fucking menace. Put us in jail, it will be safer there anyway."

"What do you mean safer?" Carter asks, and this time Chuck replies.

"You don't think we were hiding from you, do you?" He snorts and stumbles under Carter's and Kerry's grips. "Someone put a hit on us. Pretty sure it's that bitch who first hired us. If we can't testify, she will walk free."

Nolan scoffs. "No, she won't. There's always Glory."

Both brothers stare at him with derision before turning their gazes on me.

"We're not the only ones with a hit out on us."

Chapter Fourteen

little while later, the brothers are on their way to custody with the rest of the team, and I'm in the back of one of the Wrathful Bail Bonds trucks with Carter and Nolan, heading to get another fugitive. We've come to a silent agreement not to discuss my new mate and possible hit, waiting until this job is finished. We can't let anything distract us, because that's when mistakes happen. The previous bust is a perfect example.

"Okay, Glory, give us the rundown on the guy we're after," Carter tells me as he drives us toward the bar.

I look down at the rap sheet. "Mason James, aka Easter Bunny, is twenty-eight and charged with theft. He is allegedly responsible for…" I trail off as I read the charges. "Oh wow, he's allegedly responsible for the theft of over ten Fabergé eggs from various collections around the world. He was due to stand trial a week ago and never showed up, but he also wasn't hard to track. It's almost like he wants to be caught." A frown crosses my face as I remember how easy this guy was to find. It was my case to work through, and after a little searching, I found him staying in an apartment above a biker hangout.

"The bar is owned by the Savage Knights Motorcycle Club, and apparently, he is an honorary member, patched but not required to contribute to everyday club life. The president of the club is Theodore Williams, better known as Temple. Huh, I wonder why they call him that. Maybe the Shirley Temple is his signature drink."

The guys snort with amusement in the front seat.

"Temple and Easter Bunny have a connection, but I wasn't able to figure out what that was. Apparently, the only way to get to the apartment is through the bar, which means going through the Savage Knights to get to him."

"Crap," Nolan exclaims, but Carter fidgets a little in his seat before sighing and shaking his head.

"No, it's okay, I actually know the president," Carter admits.

"What?" Nolan sounds surprised and takes his eyes off the road to look at him incredulously before turning back to the road.

Carter runs a hand through his hair. "Temple is a member of the club, but because of his preferences, he asked me to keep his membership a secret."

"What do you mean by preferences?" I ask, curious as fuck.

"Temple is a bi sub, and as president of an MC,

that doesn't really fit the image. His old man was a fucking asshole, and they were one of the most ruthless MC clubs around. The old man was killed by a rival gang, and Temple took over. Under his rule, the club has given up some of the more unsavory things that they used to do, but not everyone in the club is happy about it, so his presidency is uneasy."

Okay, wow!

"Fuck, man, so we are going into a potentially hostile environment? One that has had no qualms about using guns in the past to solve problems?" Nolan sounds uneasy and looks at me in the rearview mirror. "Maybe it would be best if you stayed in the car."

We pull into a parking lot across the road from Bloody Sword Tavern, and the three of us jump out of the car. Nolan and Carter head to the back and pull out bulletproof vests and put them on before checking their Tasers and guns.

"Come on, let me go," I beg, and they both shake their heads.

"No, Glory, you're a distraction, and we'll be more worried about you and not as aware of what's going on. You're our weakness."

I cross my arms in annoyance. "Are you going to sideline me every time we do this? If so, maybe I need to work with a different team, one that isn't as invested in my safety, otherwise what was the point of all this? Were you just indulging me and hoping that I would go back to food blogging?"

"No, baby, no." Carter comes over and pulls me against his chest, wrapping his arms around me. "You're good at this and an asset to our team. How about you keep an eye on the outside? There's a fire escape from the apartment. Head around there and watch. Mason has never shown any violent tendencies in the past, according to his file, so the likelihood that he's carrying a weapon is small. It's the rest of the MC members I'm concerned about."

Slightly appeased by his words and his warm hug, I grab a vest of my own and check my weapons. "Fine, but this better not become a habit. I'm not afraid to use Sparky on the two of you again."

They both blanch, and I don't blame them. We all got a turn of feeling the Taser a few weeks back, and that shit hurt.

The three of us cross the road, and I leave them at the front of the tavern and head around to the side and down an alley where I can see a fire escape from the top floor. The alley is a dead end. There's a dumpster pushed up against the wall of the tavern that's slightly in front of the fire escape, so I could stand behind it and no one at the top could see me.

I position myself there. There's a convenient milk crate that I tip over and use to sit on while I wait. My heart races a little bit as I run through all the things in my head that could be going on inside, thinking about what the connection between our egg thief and the president of this club is. I couldn't figure out how they knew each other. They went to different schools, grew up in different areas, and didn't go to the same gyms. I'm at a loss.

Resting my elbows on my knees, I put my chin in my hands and stare down at the ground while listening for movement on the fire escape. Scuffing my foot along the ground, I think about this morning's bust. I'm relieved that the brothers are going to be behind bars, but their parting words worried me. Thankfully the girls have no clue their mother was responsible for our kidnapping. Hiding them in that shed protected them in more ways than one. There's no need for her to get rid of them as witnesses as well as me, but I wouldn't put it past her. She has no mothering instinct at all, and they are just a means to an end for her, so I don't think she would blink if she had to get rid of them too.

My thoughts wander to my new mate, and I lift my chin so I can see the latest ring around my mark. Fuck! I thought I was done. It is unusual to have more than one mate unless you're a lust demon, and I'm predominantly gluttony, or so I thought. Finding out Mom is Lucifer's sister and that he's my uncle is something I've been avoiding thinking about, but I guess she needs to be confronted. How did Kerry know that but none of my guys did? Unless she left Hell before any of them were born, which I guess is possible, and

Kerry probably knows because she grew up in Lucifer's palace. I wonder if Lucifer has mates and how many. I must ask Kerry.

My new mate didn't look too thrilled to be mated to me, though she certainly perked up when she saw Carter and Nolan. Talk about a kick in the gut. My mate is more interested in them than me. Can the universe get it wrong? Maybe I will be dissolving a mating after all, just not the one I thought I was going to.

A noise high above me has me jumping in surprise. I reach for my Taser and tuck myself behind the dumpster. I can make out quiet voices, but I can't hear what they are saying. Damn it, there's more than one. Shit, what am I going to do? I don't have my earpiece in to let the other two know, because I took it out after the drag bar and never put it back in.

The grinding of metal echoes through the alley as the fire escape ladder is lowered, and I hear whoever it is climbing down. I can't even risk peeking around the dumpster to see who it is, I'll just have to wait. My breathing becomes faster, and my blood pumps as adrenaline starts to course through my veins. I have a couple of zip ties in my pockets to restrain them if needed.

The sound of shoes on metal stops, so I'm assuming they hit the ground. Sure enough, the thud of footsteps starts to move toward me, and the quiet, urgent whispers reach my ears.

"They must be parked out front somewhere. We'll just wait across the street until they come out and approach them then," I hear one voice say.

They can't be talking about Nolan and Carter, can they? It's almost like they want to be caught.

I decide I can't wait any longer, otherwise they may pass me, and then they'll have a free run to the exit. I jump around the dumpster, but I don't get a chance to lift my Taser because I leap straight into a brick wall, and we both go down like a sack of bricks. Fuck, that's the second time today I've ended up on the ground on top of someone.

Looking up, I suck in a breath as my eyes meet the most perfect emerald green gaze. His hands come up to steady me, grabbing my arms, and once more, I get a pain in my hand. When I look down in shock, another ring is around my mate mark. How does this keep happening to me? This time it's yellow—greed demon. I guess that makes sense if this is Mason, aka Easter Bunny, but what is he doing in the human system? Usually demons are punished by Lucifer.

"Mason James, you didn't appear for your court date and are in breach of your bail conditions. You are to be remanded back into the custody of the sheriff's department while they decide your fate."

I roll off of him and hold out my hand to help him up, but I keep one hand on my Taser and an eye on the other person behind him. He stands up and brushes himself off. He's wearing jeans and a shirt, and he's tall like the rest of my mates. His hair is a similar color to mine, and longish on top but not to his shoulders, and it's pushed back from his face.

"You're my mate?" he questions, looking me up and down while ignoring my well-rehearsed speech.

After this morning's debacle, I'm not feeling particularly patient. I turn him around, grab his hands, and pull them behind his back, and before he can realize what I'm doing, I have them zip tied. I turn him back around to face me. He's wearing an amused look, and his eyes sparkle with humor.

"Do you have a problem with that?" I ask, immediately defensive again.

"Fuck no, you're hot." He grins, and a small part of my hurt heals. "But if you wanted to tie me up, you could have just asked. Between you and me, though, I'd prefer to be the one doing the tying up. Just saying."

"Ah, no offense, and I'm happy you found your mate and all, but can we get the fuck out of here? They are going to bash down that door any minute now and come after us." The gravelly voice of the man behind Mason has me looking his way, and my eyes widen with surprise.

This man is the stereotypical hot biker. His long hair is tied back in a ponytail, and he has rugged good looks that are softened by his plump lips. He's wearing a leather vest with nothing underneath it, and his arms are covered in tattoos. He's tall, like

Mason, but has a heavier build, and he looks like he could bench-press me.

"Who are you talking about? The other bond agents? You don't seem like you wanted to escape that badly." I sound skeptical, and Mason shakes his head.

"No. I wanted you to capture me. I don't want to be in the human system. I want to plead my case to Lucifer," he explains, causing me to frown. "The bond agents didn't make it upstairs. I heard gunshots, but I'm not sure what happened to them."

Fuck, I hope they are okay. Their mate marks have not faded, so they aren't dead, but that's all I can think about at the moment.

"Then who are you worried about? Who's going to bash down your door?" Just as I say this, the window above us explodes outwards, and glass rains down into the alley. Climbing out of the now open space is a leather-clad man, and he has a gun in his hand.

"Fuck, we need to go." Mason grins at me and pulls his hands apart, snapping the zip ties. Of course they are not going to hold a demon. He grabs my arm and starts to hurry us down the alley. We don't get far before a gunshot rings out and a bullet hits the wall near us, causing a piece of brick to chip off and fly toward my face, narrowly missing my eye. I cry out in shock, and Mason drags me a little faster.

"What the fuck is going on? Why are they shooting at us?" I scream as we leave the alley and run across the street, dodging the light traffic.

"Well, it looks like Temple here might have just lost his position as president, and they'd like to get rid of the evidence," Mason muses, not fazed by the gunfire at all.

Temple just grunts.

"I'm sure once they catch sight of Miss Luxure here, they will start aiming their guns at her, seeing as the hit put out on her is a large amount."

I look at Temple in shock. "How do you know who I am?"

Again, he grunts. "Hit requests usually come with a photo so you know you're killing the right person."

I can't tell if he's being sarcastic or not.

I'm stunned into silence, and when we make it across the road, I realize I can't open the car doors because Carter has the keys. I turn back to look at the tavern just as the front doors slam open, and Carter and Nolan start running toward the vehicle.

When they get to it, they look a little bemused to see the other two men with me, but we don't have time for explanations, because there are three bikers stalking out of the alleyway with their guns held high, uncaring about anyone else who may be caught in the crossfire. We jump in with Mason between Temple and me, and Carter and Nolan take the front. The tires squeal as Carter peels out of the parking lot as bullets rain down on the back of the vehicle.

"Head down, Glory," Nolan orders, and I feel Mason's hand on the back of my head before my face is in his lap.

Well, that escalated quickly. I snort in amusement despite the situation and give him back some of his own medicine. "Now, Mason, if you wanted my face in your lap, all you had to do was ask, but I'd prefer it if we both had our faces in each other's laps."

The car is silent before I hear snorts and chuckles from the men around me.

Silence means the bullets have stopped, so I sit back up and turn around, looking behind us. The bikers haven't given chase, and we have gotten away relatively unharmed.

"Are you guys alright?" I ask my two mates in front.

"Yes, are you?" Nolan turns to look at me, and Carter watches me in the rearview mirror while rubbing his mate mark.

Both of them felt that I found another mate.

Nolan pulls his phone out of his pocket, and I watch as his fingers fly across the screen. "I'm just letting Louis know everything is alright." He puts it back into his pocket and looks at the two guys in the back seat with me. "I think we all need to have an adult conversation. Don't you?"

Mason grins and nods, but Temple just grunts again. He's a man of few words, that one.

I breathe out a big sigh. Today has been a lot, and I close my eyes for the journey to the office. I need to sort out my feelings so I can approach this with calm logic.

Chapter Fifteen

By the time we arrive back at Wrathful Bail Bonds, I'm exhausted. Too much has gone on in such a short amount of time. I just want to go home, climb into my bed, and pull the covers up over my head.

Confronting the guys, the take down of the two brothers, finding two new mates, and having a hit put out on me has all been too much—not to mention I still haven't found out why my brothers are now all working at Garden of Eden.

I trudge up the stairs to Carter and Nolan's office, my body, head, and heart heavy with emotions. The others are in front of me, and the silence between the four of them is adding to my tension. We don't see anyone else as we move through the floor. The rest of the class is out shadowing other teams or down in the gun range, working on their marksman skills. Carter called ahead to make sure that the floor was cleared out before we got here. We don't need humans overhearing demon business, nor do we want them to be suspicious when they see Mason without cuffs on.

Carter closes the door behind me, since I'm the

last to enter the room, and gives my shoulder a little squeeze before moving around to the other side of the desk with Nolan. Both of them stand with their arms crossed, wearing fearsome expressions on their faces. I throw myself onto the couch and leave Mason and Temple standing.

"First, I want to hear from you" —Nolan points to Mason— "and then you can enlighten us on your situation." He looks at Temple who nods. "What the fuck were you thinking, stealing such high-profile things and from such a high-profile exhibit? How did you manage to get caught, and why haven't you been collected by Lucifer's team for punishment?"

Mason takes one of the remaining empty chairs and leans back in it, a cocky grin on his face. He makes a performance of stretching and putting his arms behind his head before he answers. I hear three growls from the remaining men in the room. None of them are impressed with his antics, and I can't say I am either, but he does have nice fore-arms, just saying.

"Now those are a lot of very good questions which require a multitude of answers."

Oh no, dude. That's not the way to go about it. That's only going to get his ass kicked. Sure enough, someone reacts, and it's not the two I thought it would be. Temple cuffs his friend—are they friends? I'm not sure—across the head, and that certainly gets a reaction.

Mason drops the act and sits up straight, looking at his friend in shock. "You hit me?" He sounds surprised, and then Temple does something that stuns the rest of us.

He drops to his knees with his head bowed and shakes with emotion. "I'm sorry, sir, but this is important, and these people can hopefully help both of us."

Oh, yup, definitely more than just friends. Shit, that was the connection I was missing. I didn't think to look at Carter's club for one.

Mason reaches out and places his hand on Temple's shoulder. "Shh, it's okay, I know you're stressed. This time it will be overlooked, but not again."

I fan my face as I watch the two of them, my mind going to places that it really shouldn't at the moment. Fuck, poor Temple, he probably doesn't have a clue about demons and mates, but then as he reaches up, grabs Mason's arm, and squeezes it in gratitude, I catch sight of his hand. Sitting in the little bit of skin between the thumb and pointer finger is a purple mark. Huh, he's a pride demon. That's kind of weird, considering he's a sub. I would have thought that it went against everything in him.

Carter and Nolan look as confused as I feel. Mason sighs, and the joking man disappears, replaced by someone serious.

"The Fabergé egg I stole contains the soul of an

ex-lover of mine. When he and I went our separate ways, he took up with a less than savory group of demons—ones who are into dark magic and shit. They use blood sacrifices and have powers that are not demonic in nature. He realized how much shit he was in, but by then it was too late. His new lover, Mabuz, was obsessed, and he decided that if he couldn't have him, then no one could. Mabuz killed him and then imprisoned his soul in the Gatchina Palace egg, which was on display at the museum where I was caught. He thought it was ironic that the egg contained an extra surprise that all Fabergé eggs were said to contain." He looks distraught, and I can understand why. No one likes the thought of a soul being trapped, especially a previous love.

"So how did you get caught though? Why didn't you muddle their minds?" Apart from being able to conjure shit, that is the other main power a demon possesses. A few of the more powerful ones have extra abilities, like Lucifer who can teleport, but most of us are just average Joes in the power stakes.

"It was a trap set by the demon who imprisoned him. Mabuz knew I'd been asking around and had discovered what happened, so I set off the museum's alarms at the same time, and their security arrived before the demon and carted me away. Otherwise, I'm pretty sure my soul would have ended up inside that egg too."

"Why did you let us catch you?" Carter still has his arms crossed, and he's frowning with distrust.

Mason shrugs. "Because I needed to get Lucifer's attention, otherwise I would have been lost in the system." He holds his hand up, and a pretty, decorative egg appears in it. "I also need his help releasing Matius's soul." The light hits the enamel on the side of the egg, making it shine brightly.

"Whoa, that's so pretty." The gluttony demon inside of me is screaming with want, but I place my hands under my legs so I don't reach for it. Mason's eyes meet mine, and they sparkle with the same kind of want. Greed and gluttony demons aren't so different from one another.

"The reason I was able to get bail was because I didn't have the egg on me. I had just enough time to send it to Temple's apartment before security arrived. I told them that it was empty when I got there and was able to muddle the cameras enough to make it seem like it could have been. My case will probably be thrown out, but then the demon who did this will be after me to get the egg back, and I can't let that happen." The egg in his hand disappears once more, returning to whatever safe space he kept it in.

Nolan and Carter exchange glances then both look at Temple.

"What about you? How are you involved with all this? I didn't recognize Mason because he's always wearing a mask. I think it might have been different if he'd been wearing less clothes," Carter admits candidly.

Hmm, I wonder if he ever fed off their desire when they were in his club. *Damn it, Glory, get your head out of the gutter.* "So I now understand how the two of you are involved, but what the fuck was with the MC members? I thought you were the President of the club."

Temple looks to Mason for permission to move, and Mason gives him another squeeze on the shoulder before nodding. Temple gets to his feet before running a hand through his hair, pulling it out of its neat ponytail. He tugs on it a couple of times before taking a seat next to Mason.

"After my birth father died when I was a baby, my mother went a little wild. Losing a mate is never easy, and combined with postpartum depression, well, she latched onto the first man who paid any interest to her, and that just so happened to be the president of the Savage Knights MC club. He wasn't interested in having a baby around, so for the first ten years of my life, I was raised by my maternal grandmother, but she died not long after I turned ten, and I was returned to my mother's custody. On the outside, she looked perfectly respectable to CPS, with a steady job and a home and a husband, but it was all a lie." I watch as the light in his eyes fades as he gets lost in his story. "She worked for the MC club in the bar you found us at, but she wasn't a bartender. She was a whore, a lure. When she wasn't spreading her legs, she would go around to clubs pretending to be a modeling talent scout and lure in young women with the promise of fame. They would then disappear, sold to the sex trafficking ring the Savage Knights ran. Kenneth, or Killer, as he was called in the club, kept her on a short leash, giving her enough drugs to keep her addicted and coming back, but not too much that she wasn't able to function. In her twisted mind, though, she was proud of how successful she was at both jobs."

The lump in my throat is hard to swallow around as Temple's sordid childhood is narrated to us, his voice dull and lifeless as he remembers the horror.

"My mother wasn't able to have any more children because my birth required her to have a hysterectomy at the same time, so when I came to live with them at the age of ten, he took me under his wing. He scared the fuck out of me and beat me thoroughly until I had no choice but to do what I was told. He also said that he would kill my mom, but by that stage, I couldn't have cared less, because she hadn't once stopped him. In fact, she laughed and told him to dirty her pathetic son up a little more." His voice breaks off, and Mason reaches for his hand, giving him a squeeze of encouragement.

"When I was in middle school, I was expected to peddle drugs for him, and by the time I was fourteen, since I hadn't developed a taste for the whoring, violent ways of the club, he decided that if I was such a pussy, I could be sold like one too. He sold me to men and women who had a liking for younger men. I wasn't quite a child, but I wasn't a man either. He would give me drugs to perform and hold a gun to my head if I didn't. Eventually, I realized that unless I played along and became the monster he wanted me to be, I wouldn't be able to get away. During one such session with one of the foulest men he sold me to, I fought back. I'm not sure if he fucked up the dose or my demon genes pushed the drugs through my system faster, but I was coherent. I fought the man off me and tackled Kenneth, surprising him, and wrestled the gun out of his grasp. I unloaded the whole magazine into the creep who raped me. I instantly regretted not saving one for Kenneth. I knew that was it, and I was about to die, but as I turned and faced my fate, I found him laughing his head off and clapping his hands. He said, 'You are finally showing me the stuff that a true knight is made of.' He clapped me on the shoulder, and the next day, I was patched as a member. I had to do some truly awful things for that man, but I soon won his trust, and after he named me his successor, I took care of him."

Temple took a deep breath before continuing. "The next time we were in a gunfight with a rival gang, I put a bullet in his skull and blamed the other gang. Nobody was the wiser. I've spent the last couple of years trying to reel in the criminal activities of the gang, including abandoning the sex trafficking ring, but the members are not happy. I knew a coup was coming." He turns to look at me, his brown eyes so dark they are almost black. "When I refused the hit on Glory, I knew that was the last straw. The rumbles of discontent couldn't be contained, and I had just enough time to make it up to the apartment before shit hit the fan. You must have walked into the bar just after I escaped."

The silence is heavy around the office as he finishes his story, his eyes still locked on mine. A heavy sigh leaves Nolan's mouth, and Temple turns to look at him.

"The person who took out the hit was Bridgette Weston. Does that ring a bell?"

Fuck, the brothers were right. Bridgette is out for revenge in the worst possible way.

Carter and Nolan explode in a litany of curses, and Carter picks up a stapler before hurling it at the wall in anger. Mason, Temple, and I watch on in silence, not wanting to get in the way. I'm just going to let them have their moment, but after the first outburst, Nolan became very quiet. I study him carefully. His wrath demon is suspiciously absent in his eyes—this is not a good sign.

"Nolan, are you okay?" I ask cautiously, and this has Carter stopping and looking at him too.

"Nolan, man, you need to get to the gym and beat the shit out of the bags, otherwise you're going to explode, and we are going to get caught in the crossfire," Carter warns.

Nolan doesn't say a word or look anywhere. He

just moves around his desk and pulls open the office door with so much force, he yanks it off the hinges. Fuck, he's mad. He carefully leans it up against the wall and leaves the office.

A sigh of relief escapes Carter's mouth before he turns to me. "Glory, take Mason and Temple to our place. They can stay in one of the spare rooms for now while I deal with Nolan. I think the best bet for all of us is to move to Hell until this can be sorted. You and the girls will be safe, Mason can speak to Lucifer about releasing the soul, and we can ask Kerry's dad for help in finding Bridgette. She must be getting assistance from someone. Nolan and I have been searching for her and haven't found a single breadcrumb of a trail. Maybe we can interrogate the lawyer. He might know where she is, and someone has to be putting up the money for the hit, because we know she's broke."

Neither Mason nor Temple argue with anything Carter suggests. In fact, they both look relieved. Standing up, I go over to my lust mate and give him a kiss. I can tell by the way he latches on to me that he needs energy. He's not the only one. I reluctantly pull away and caress his cheek with my hand.

"Hurry home so one or all of us can help you out." I move away and gesture for Mason and Temple to follow.

Temple still looks morose, but Mason is staring

at me with a sparkle in his eye, and he winks when he sees me looking.

"Before you deal with Nolan, can you call Louis and let him know what is going on please? Ask him to order food for all of us and extra for me, then call my mom and have her bring the girls straight home," I say. "Oh, and you're going to have to ask Sam and Dean to take over the class for now while we're away and let them know they are going to have to order new gym equipment, since I'm sure there won't be much left of it when Nolan is done."

Carter's eyes sparkle in amusement at all my orders, and I'm aware I've gone into bossy mode, but it's my way of coping and avoiding all the other issues going on in my life.

"Yes, boss," he teases as I lead Mason and Temple out of the room.

"And don't you forget it," I shout back as we walk away, swinging my hips.

I feel Mason sidle up next to me, his hand reaching out and caressing my ass. "They might let you boss them around, but don't think that will work with me. I can't wait to see your plump ass pink with my handprints," he growls in my ear, and I feel my nipples pebble in response as I push his hands off.

"A bit presumptuous, aren't you?" I retort sassily. "I like it when they dominate me in the bedroom, so I'm not sure if I have a need for another, but I wouldn't say no to a submissive." I turn and wink at Temple who jolts in surprise and then smirks. I feel Mason stop, and when I turn, I find him speechless. "Well, it's nice to know you can be shut up," I call as I descend the stairs toward the exit, putting a little extra sway into my step just for him.

When we arrive home, the house is in chaos.

Max is bouncing around and barking like crazy because my mother didn't just drop the girls off—oh no, Mom has to stick her nose into everything. She's throwing her arms around and demanding for a very harassed-looking Louis to tell her what's going on. The girls are dancing around him, trying to tell him all about their day, and shouting over the top of my mom. My normally very put together French mate looks like a mess. He's wearing track pants that are hanging low on his hips and a wife beater, and his hair is sticking up in all angles as if he has been running his hand through it nonstop. The poor man was on night shift last night, and I guess he didn't get much sleep today, not to mention he would have felt both new matings.

A sharp whistle by my side has everyone stopping and looking in our direction. I nod to Mason in thanks, and he winks at me again.

Louis's eyes light up in relief when he sees me. "Glory, my little tea kettle, thank God you are home. I have been so worried." His accent is thick with concern, and he pushes past my mother to rush toward me and gather me in his arms. "Thank fuck you're home, your mother is a menace," he whispers in my ear, and I snort. He pulls away and looks over my shoulder. "Are these your two new mates?"

I turn back to look at them too. "Nope, just the one." I wave at Mason, and he winks at Louis. "Mason is one of the fugitives we had to chase down today."

Louis doesn't look surprised, so I figure Carter has already called and filled him in, but I hear my mom screech in dismay, and I roll my eyes.

"The other one is his…" Friend? Boyfriend? Sub? "The other one is Temple," I finish, unsure how to explain the situation, and with little ears in hearing range, it's best to just leave it at that for now.

"I can't believe that you are chasing down criminals, Gloriana." My mother lets her annoyance be heard by one and all, but I ignore her and scoop my girls up into a big hug.

They both giggle and try to tell me all about their day, but I overhear Louis invite Mason and Temple to sit, and that gets their attention. They stop trying to talk to me and eye the two men warily.

"Who are they, Mom?" Aria asks suspiciously.

Zoe sticks her thumb in her mouth and stares at them wide-eyed.

"Oh, um, they are our new friends. They are going to be staying here for a while," I reply.

Zoe takes her thumb out of her mouth and looks at Mason. "You're pretty."

The man preens at the compliment from the three-year-old. I mean, she's not wrong. My three mates are hot, but Mason's looks are ridiculous, and I feel a stab of envy. He's prettier than I am. He shivers with delight as my envy pings in the air around him. Well, I'm glad I'm keeping him energized at least, which reminds me…

"Babe, did you order dinner?" I ask Louis, still ignoring my mom.

"Of course I did, my little spring roll." Louis's pet names make me smile, and I think he knows this because they seem to get more and more ridiculous.

"Great, okay, girls, why don't you run upstairs and wash up for dinner while I get rid of… say goodbye to Grandma."

They both do as I instructed and run off upstairs to get ready for dinner.

"Stop, Mom!" I tell her firmly.

She has spent the last few minutes pacing back and forth, muttering to herself in French. Louis looks at her with laughter in his eyes, so I can't wait to hear what she has to say.

"I will not!" she declares with a gasp. "My

daughter's a bounty hunter. I never!" She sounds indignant.

"Mom, your other daughter is a whore, get over it."

She gasps and holds her hand up to her chest like I've wounded her. "Being a whore is one of the oldest and most honest professions in the world, and it's perfect for her. Why can't you just go back to food blogging? You were so good at it," she coos, trying to convince me, but I shake my head.

"Mom, just stop. It's not going to happen, but while you're here, what's this I hear about Lucifer being your brother?"

She pales and collapses into the armchair behind her. "How did you find out?"

"One of the girls in my class is from Hell. Her father is the head of Lucifer's enforcement squad, so she grew up in the palace. Apparently, Lucifer talks about his sister Petra all the time and often laments that she is no longer with him."

She blushes with shame and looks down at her lap, wringing her hands. "Yes, Lucifer is my brother and your uncle. I'm afraid I made some stupid mistakes when I was younger and, well, instead of admitting I was wrong, I chose to hold a grudge. It has been many years since I have returned home. Your fathers haven't even met my brother. It's the one true regret I have with my life. That, and not interacting with demon society more and introducing you kids to it. That was my stubborn pride, and I thought if I avoided Hell, then I could forget the stupid mistakes I made."

"Oh, Mom." I go over and wrap my arm around her shoulders as tears stream down her face. "Whatever happened, I'm sure you and your brother can work things out."

She wipes at the tears on her face and vehemently shakes her head. "Don't be so sure. I made a mistake and was taken in by a lover. He convinced me that he was my mate and the marks just hadn't appeared yet. I was blinded by my lust and thirst for this demon. He convinced me to give him Lucifer's most sacred book of magic—magic so powerful that all but a few have been forbidden to know it. Only Luc and his three trusted lieutenants have ever seen the inside of the pages until I gave it to Mabuz."

I gasp as the name leaves her lips and look at Mason, who is also stunned. I can't believe this is all interconnecting.

"As soon as he had his hands on the book, he disappeared, leaving me heartbroken and feeling foolish. When my brother confronted me, instead of admitting that I was wrong, I accused him of not giving me the power of the book to allow me to protect myself. I told him that he was selfish and greedy, and had he shared, I might not have fallen for Mabuz's tricks."

My mom growls, and she's lost in the memory as her hands ball into fists. "He was calm and patient and maddening. I just wanted to hit him.

Even through all my ranting, he stayed calm and didn't rise to the bait, and when I finally ran out of steam, he calmly told me I was not ready for such power."

She sighs in defeat. "He was right, and in the end, I left Hell in shame, but when I got to Earth, I was alone, lonely, and starving. Although demons visit Earth, not many of them permanently live here. They will for a few years, but all will eventually go home and have families, so I started the Palace of Sinful Delights as a way to feed and provide a service for demons who hadn't found their mates. Most demons don't like to have flings with humans because they can result in children, so I employed demon girls and guys for visiting demons to have fun with. It was a good employment opportunity for those who wanted to play earthside for a few years before settling down. Since demons are not as tied down with morals as humans, they didn't even blink at becoming paid sex workers. Most of them think it's awesome they get paid to have sex."

I know much of what Mom is saying. I guess it's for the other people in the room, but I know none of them are judging her.

"That's when I met your three fathers. When I mated them, I stopped seeing other demons."

"Well, Mom, I think you're going to have to swallow your pride and reach out to him. I need a place for all of us to hide. Nolan's ex has gone insane and taken out a hit on my life, and she seems to have disappeared. Nolan and Carter want to ask Lucifer's demon guard to help find her. They are unable to concentrate on it as much as they would like because they are worried about me and the girls."

"With good reason. The hit said that it didn't matter if the girls were taken out in the crossfire," Temple adds, his disgust evident on his face.

The growl that escapes Louis's mouth is unlike anything I've ever heard from him before.

"That monster!" Oh dear, Bridgette has done it now. She threatened the lives of the girls, so Petra will be on the warpath. She stands up, straightens her outfit, and waves her hand in front of her face, removing all signs of her tears. "I will head to Hell and grovel to my brother if I need to. Anything to protect my family." Mom gives Louis and me a kiss, and with a curt head nod to the other two, she disappears out the front door.

"How does one get to Hell?" I muse out loud, and Mason grins.

"There are portals in all Walmarts. You know the changing room that is always out of order?"

I nod, knowing how much that pisses me off.

"Well, that's the portal. It makes it convenient here in the US. It's the same in certain chain department stores around the world."

Huh.

I drum my fingers on my thigh, and my foot

jiggles up and down. This day has been a cluster-fuck. The doorbell rings before I can worry about anything else, and I stand up. That must be the Chinese food.

"Louis, can you show Mason and Temple to rooms or a room? I don't know, but I'm sure you can all sort it out. I'll grab the food."

The others stand up, but as I pass Mason, he grabs my arm. "You and I need to talk. I have questions," he tells me, all the cockiness gone from his tone.

"Yes, we do." I look between him and Temple. "But not now, and not today. It's been too much," I plead with him, and his eyes soften with sympathy.

He nods and follows Temple and Louis, leaving me to answer the door.

When I pull it open, I find a man standing there, but he's not holding any food in his hand. He's tall, with short black hair and gray eyes that are lined with kohl. He has cheekbones that would make my mother weep and plump lips any woman would be jealous of. He's wearing a faded pair of blue jeans and a T-shirt that stretches across his slender body. While Mason is pretty, he's still manly, but this man is pretty and borders on being effeminate.

I frown in confusion. "Can I help you?" I ask him, peering around him to see if he left the food in the car, but a black BMW is sitting there, and I certainly can't smell any Chinese. I meet his gray eyes.

"Hi, I'm Ben," he says in a quiet, gentle voice, and I wrinkle my nose in confusion. "Nolan and Carter told me to come on over."

"Well, yes, that's usually what Chinese delivery does." It's like he finally realizes what I'm talking about.

"Oh no, I'm not the delivery guy." He strikes a pose and assumes a different voice. "I'm Poppy Cox, your new mate, darling."

Holy crap, the drag queen. I'm trying to find the words to apologize for the confusion when I hear a crack, and seconds later, a piece of brick peels off the doorway, slicing across my face for the second time today.

"Fuck, shots!" Poppy/Ben screams and tackles me to the ground, and we find ourselves in the same position as this morning, only reversed.

Two more shots hit next to the door when Temple comes running outside, holding what looks like a freaking machine gun. He sprays a barrage of bullets in the direction the shots came from—somewhere near the edge of the property amongst the trees.

The gunfire stops, and the silence around us is deadly. I can hear the girls crying inside while Louis tries to comfort them. A few seconds later, we hear the sounds of tires squealing and a car being driven away at high speed.

I tear my eyes away from Temple and look up at the man lying on top of me.

"And here I thought being mated was going to make my life boring. Well, sugar, you certainly blew that out of the water." He sounds breathless but excited at the same time.

Oh, Poppy, you have no idea.

Acknowledgments

Grace and Hope. My throuple members, my author wife and PA, my best bitches—Jesus this was a hard one and if it wasn't for the two of you it would never have gotten written. But on the flip side because of the two of you, the story grew and now I need to write another two books as opposed to just one. So thanks a lot assholes.

To Jillian and Kerry, thanks for jumping and helping me out with alpha reading, I love you guys.

To my super awesome beta team, your help is as always much appreciated.

To my cover designer Tash, of Dazed Designs. Thank you for making the covers exactly what I envisioned, you are amazing.

Thank you to Jillian at Locke and Key Proof-reading.

Thank Jessica from elemental Editing as usual you rock!

As much as I struggled with this one I am really happy with the way it turned out. Imagine my surprise when Glory ended up with more mates though. I had thought she was done with only three of the first book but no that bitch truly is gluttonous.

Lexie